Dear Susan
Thanks for everything right through the years
Claire x

First published by Amazon 2023

Copyright © 2023 by Claire Keogh

All rights reserved. No part of this publication may be reproduced, stored or transmitted in any form or by any means, electronic, mechanical, photocopying, recording, scanning, or otherwise without written permission from the publisher. It is illegal to copy this book, post it to a website, or distribute it by any other means without permission.

This novel is entirely a work of fiction. The names, characters and incidents portrayed in it are the work of the author's imagination. Any resemblance to actual persons, living or dead, events or localities is entirely coincidental.

Claire Keogh asserts the moral right to be identified as the author of this work.

Designations used by companies to distinguish their products are often claimed as trademarks. All brand names and product names used in this book and on its cover are trade names, service marks, trademarks and registered trademarks of their respective owners. The publishers and the book are not associated with any product or vendor mentioned in this book. None of the companies referenced within the book have endorsed the book.

First edition

This book was professionally typeset on Reedsy.
Find out more at reedsy.com

Contents

Chapter 1	1
Chapter 2	10
Chapter 3	15
Chapter 4	20
Chapter 5	24
Chapter 6	30
Chapter 7	35
Chapter 8	41
Chapter 9	46
Chapter 10	51
Chapter 11	56
Chapter 12	63
Chapter 13	68
Chapter 14	73
Chapter 15	75
Chapter 16	79
Chapter 17	84
Chapter 18	88
Chapter 19	91
Chapter 20	94
Chapter 21	97
Chapter 22	105
Chapter 23	108
Chapter 24	113
Chapter 25	117
Chapter 26	119

Chapter 27	122
Chapter 28	124
Chapter 29	130
Chapter 30	134
Post Script	140

Chapter 1

It was busy in London on a September Monday morning at six. For some people, six is the perfect time for an early morning workout in the gym or the perfect time to go jogging in the park on the streets near Wimbledon Common. The streets can be full of students who are stressing about going back to their colleges, universities, and schools after the summer break.

The streets can be full of shoppers planning their carefree summer sunshine evenings. Or they can be full of people who are just going about their daily business, even at that hour. Shopkeepers opening their businesses, hoping for a brisk day's trade and bus drivers and schoolteachers going about their work, while street cleaners clear what is left of the nightly rubbish.

For Irene Harley and Gary Russell, this was just a normal day. Coming into town from their small, mortgaged apartment, on an Underground line with their twin Oyster cards, they worked on opposite sides of the same street in the heart of the financial district.

Gary was an associate at a law firm, and Irene was a secretary for two owners in a commercial real estate company, reporting to the administration manager Suzanne Barron, who was also a partner of the firm.

"Will we meet for lunch today?" said Gary to Irene gently as he left her near her building, "or will we skip it and I'll cook dinner at home later. You have a class, don't you?"

"Mondays are busy, and I must type up meeting minutes from last week, so I'm not sure when I'll be free," replied Irene.

"Well, I'll shoot you a text at one pm and see how you're fixed. You might be able to stop working long enough for a bite to eat. You know how I worry about you."

Gary stroked Irene's hair and kissed her on the cheek. He worried she didn't eat enough and trained too hard, but she was determined not to let these things take over her life and she didn't like him fussing over her.

"I'll eat when I'm hungry, Gary, you're such a fusspot," she would say.

The pair had met after an online introduction and had moved in together in what appeared to be a whirlwind romance within a matter of weeks.

They were besotted with each other soon after meeting having set up a date following a brief flurry of messages.

Their first meeting was a walk around the park and an ice-cream between their various respective activities. It hardly seemed likely that either of them had time for romance, but they both appeared to want to make it work, or so it seemed.

Two years after their first date, Irene was now twenty-five-years-old, petite, and brown-haired, brimming with confidence in her job at the firm. Getting together with Gary had been good for her, as she had suffered a little with anxiety during college.

Now, she was sporty, and enjoyed five-a-side soccer and swimming which she had always loved from her earliest years. In fact, her dad said she could swim before she could walk. Despite many people ending up in jobs they didn't love, for Irene, the secretary's job in the commercial real estate office was exactly what she wanted at that point in time.

Although she appeared junior to many, it hadn't been easy to get a job where she was valued the way she was; having only a two-year business administration degree when most people seeking jobs in London offices her age had master's degrees.

But she was smart and sassy, and she hoped to climb straight up the ladder once she was ready. Besides, secretaries earned decent money, and she wasn't in that much of a hurry to become a manager.

She liked her time off and holidays far too much, and she didn't want to be a slave to the partners any more than she was already. Far too many people had problems with the word *Secretary*, but Irene didn't - she knew it covered a multitude of roles and responsibilities that could be asked of her at any minute.

Gary was ten years older with classic good looks, a slightly tanned face and heavy-set jaw, and an Oxford education which led to his choice of career as a lawyer. He would do well if it hadn't been for some poor choices early on in his life before college. He was caught smoking cannabis at sixteen, and narrowly avoided a possession conviction.

His uncle was a judge and had to vouch for his character, but he made sure that Gary knew he would never do it again.

Gary had a typical public-school upbringing and a very privileged lifestyle growing up, the younger of two siblings. His brother James was three years his senior. He was the son of parents who were lawyers too, but Gary didn't get into his father's law firm, as he was not the favoured son, and he sometimes felt like he was a failure.

The privilege of being favoured was left to his brother James, with whom there was always some rivalry. James was sportier and smarter, and generally a better-liked person who had in fact become the youngest junior counsel in his father's law practise, Gary meanwhile, had still been struggling to get through law school.

Gary had felt like a failure ever since he had been beaten badly at an individual debating society event which his father had made a special effort to attend.

Does work pay, or is work an evil inflicted on a world gone mad?

He remembered that was the topic of the night in question, and argument in favour of work was torn apart by a skilled and sophisticated orator.

He thought it raised some deep philosophical issues, and he even quoted Aristotle.

"Is work really a social good? If it is such a good, is it a special one, one that

should be prioritized over others?" He remembered asking.

"Wouldn't it be fairer to let people choose their own idea of what is good for them? To get the question of whether work is really a social good into focus, it helps to specify, in suitably abstract terms, the kind of activity that work is. Aristotle did this by way of a distinction between praxis, which is action done for its own sake, and poiesis, or activity aimed at the production of something useful."

But after the debate, which he lost, his father told him he would never be a lawyer, and never mentioned taking him into the family firm again, although he did pay for his education, but nothing more.

Gary's family appeared to be too busy working and living in their own upper-class bubble to worry about Gary anymore. He appeared not to be good enough and maybe that's why he didn't spend so much time trying to communicate.

There had been an occasion in the past when Gary suspected that his dad was having an affair, and Gary confronted him. It was his dad's secretary, and shortly afterwards she left the office, and his dad became unhappy as a result.

But his mom and dad's marriage didn't break up over this, and this family anecdote may have had more to do with his apparent disfavor in the family than anything else although he didn't know exactly what he had done wrong.

James became and remained his dad's favorite son, who knew exactly how to wrap his father around his finger with manipulation tactics and was adored by his mother unreservedly.

His grades were better than Gary's at school, and he was better at networking than Gary appeared to be. So, Gary, although he was the youngest in the family, and naturally supposed to be the favorite, it didn't appear to work out that way.

Not in the Russell family anyway.

Gary got on so well with Irene because his relationship with his own family was not always the strongest. He wanted to secure a family at all costs with a particular lady who took his fancy at the time. In this case, it was Irene.

Some people might say there was too much of an age difference between Gary, at thirty-five and Irene, now twenty-five, but not to them.

Chapter 1

Who knows? Who knows anything about other people's relationships?

In the morning, the sun shone brightly as Gary and Irene gave each other a quick peck on the cheek.

Their arrangement in living together soon after they met was supposed to be temporary. But the opportunity came when both of their shared leases ended. They put a deposit on a flat in a reasonably unfashionable but still central part of London and made the joint purchase together.

Irene saw a small, classified advertisement in a local newspaper for a real estate agent who had property available, and she persuaded Gary to come and see the flat after work one day.

The building was open from three pm to five pm on a particular day and they booked an appointment to see it together. On the day in question, there was snow on the ground and the snowstorm had been forecast by the weathermen on television, and in the end nobody else showed up for the viewing. The property had been on the market for quite a while, and the price had been reduced due to water damage. But they knew this was only cosmetic and they could fix it quite easily, so they put in an offer on the property, and the vendors accepted.

"Come on Gary, it'll be good for us," she pleaded at the time. He agreed, after little persuasion.

He could see it was a good deal and he wanted to settle in his own way, but the plan was a better deal for Irene because she earned less money, and it may have been that she wouldn't have qualified for any sort of purchase on her own.

Gary was very happy to go along with the plan because he had a twelve-year-old daughter, Rosie, from an earlier relationship. He liked to have Rosie visit, and it had been difficult having her stay in shared rented accommodation prior to this.

But at the time, they were still in their honeymoon phase, getting to know each other's quirks and foibles and enjoying life. Who knows what the future might hold, what each day would bring for each of them?

Irene wondered what the morning would bring as she exited the elevator to the top floor on this September morning. Today was the first day of the week, so she had her five-a-side soccer gear with her as she played with a team from the office. Team building for the office staff and any partners who wanted to join in, they called it, but she didn't mind. In fact, she liked the idea of being in a team, both at the office and on the five-a-side.

Irene was a career lady at heart and wanted no children. She was still young, she was happy for now, and she thought that would be her lot in life. she had opened her heart to having a stepdaughter in Rosie, and she enjoyed spending time with her, but looking after herself was quite enough.

She had anxiety and was the youngest of her siblings, she had been the family favourite. The problems she appeared to have may have been an unconscious reason Gary and she connected so well. He seemed to understand her.

Irene decided a few years ago that she didn't want her own child because she didn't want to have to deal with additional drama such as this in her life.

Now, she only had time for her sports and her job, and Gary of course. Although she would barely admit it, the problems of her own were quite difficult to deal with, and barely hidden beneath the surface.

But was it fair on Gary to make this decision so early on in their joint life? She seemed to think so, and he didn't seem to mind.

At the beginning of the relationship, Irene wasn't sure that somebody like Gary with the kind of past that he had, was going to be the sort of man that would like to settle down with her, or she with him, for that matter.

In the end, it didn't prove too much of a problem, and they moved in together anyway. But as she was to find out, moving in together is only half the battle. It's only the start of a long process of building a future and a life together.

Julia was Gary's earlier partner, the mother of Rosie. She was a woman whom he had met overseas on a work trip and who later came to live with him. Their relationship had broken down suddenly, and she moved out of their rented flat. Irene had been told by Gary that Julia appeared not to be able to get work in London because her English wasn't so good, and she worked in lower paid jobs as a result. She suspected there was more to it and wondered why Gary still appeared to support them and provide financing

Chapter 1

for Julia and Rosie together.

Having said that, Julia hadn't caused much trouble in their lives so far. As long, that is, as Gary supports her and her daughter financially to the best of his ability. The financial sum wasn't that significant to him, but it must have helped Julia because it seemed to keep her happy.

He had access to his daughter every other weekend and took Rosie to the cinema and ballpark until she was too old to complain. Now at twelve, she wants to be taken to concerts at night - that's when she's not complaining that her father isn't cool enough to be seen with her.

"Come on dad I really want to see Coldplay," she would say.

"How much are the tickets?" He'd reply knowing they were very expensive.

"Dad, if you really loved me, you would buy them for me. And you can come too," she would bargain with affection.

Irene envies her boss in many respects, but she knows she's no match for her in the business world. Not yet anyway. She is happy being a secretary for the moment, more senior than some others, but always more junior than the partners and associates.

It didn't matter to Irene, she was happy, and she was loved up with Gary - for all his faults.

She often thought about how lucky she was to work at the real estate firm, but then she thought on the other hand how there were some tasks and responsibilities that she didn't like. But overall, she was happy now and didn't think it could change in an instant.

"And that counts for something in this crazy town," she thought.

How quickly things could change, she could see that side of London and office politics too. When local politics and romance were somehow connected, as they often were, and people who you had worked with just one day appeared to disappear into thin air. You might find out later that they had died, moved to a new city or county, or had transferred into another job with no warning or notice whatsoever.

In fact, an unceremonious escorting from the premises was the typical way to exit if you were asked to leave a job.

The view from the boss's office on the partners' floor and the office block on the top of the building in the financial district was spectacular. She could see for miles around the London Eye, Big Ben, the Parliament buildings, and the Palace if the sun was shining and was clear like today. In the distance, Irene could see Westminster Abbey, large and magnificent, and the boats on the River Thames.

Before long, Grace Foster, Irene's best friend in the office, who worked in accounts, stopped by her desk.

"Let's take a swim at lunchtime and work off that doughnut you're about to eat," said Grace to Irene, handing her a bag from the local doughnut shop with a cherry treat inside.

"Oh, Grace, you'll be the death of me," she laughs.

Irene, pretty and well put together, has always been a little obsessed about her appearance and particularly her weight.

She had a sweet tooth and fig rolls were her favourite, but despite this, she had managed to keep slim and trim with swimming training, gym classes, and team soccer with the guys at work. She looked good without seeming to try at all. She did try, though nobody seemed to notice the effect the trying had on her. Trying to fit in, trying to be ordinary, yet at the same time trying to be special.

She had always managed to turn heads at parties without any effort.

But her mother feared that she may have an eating disorder because of the obsession with food and exercising, and thought that she should seek counselling or go to a support group for disordered eating.

Irene wasn't having any of that kind of talk from her mother and managed to keep her mental health secure while eating normally and practising mindfulness. She listened to guided meditations over streaming waterfalls and chirping birds while she sat in a yoga pose.

Irene didn't mind that Gary had a daughter.

At least she got to know Rosie in the beginning with him.

The two of them were now living in London and their parents had separate lives in the suburbs.

Otherwise, they may never have gotten their flat. Gary and Irene had grown up moving in different social circles. By the time they met, they appeared

Chapter 1

to be well suited and moved easily in their respective professional lives – although oddly, it had been an online algorithm on a dating platform that had set them up.

"*Funny how things work out,*" Irene thought.

Appearing now to sit on top of the world carefree, life was good for Irene and Gary.

She thought aloud again, "What were chances of a mathematical algorithm on a dating website setting them up after all they had in common?"

They could easily have met on the Underground on their way to work on opposite sides of the same street in the financial district of London.

But having said that, whoever talks to strangers on the Underground?

Chapter 2

"Let's nip home early this Friday after work when Suzanne leaves," said Grace to Irene, later in the morning when they were having their coffee and doughnut on a break.

"That's a good idea. I can go shopping for a new dress for the party on Saturday at the tennis club. It's going to be a posh do. Suzanne normally leaves around two in the afternoon on a Friday for her off-site meetings, and she doesn't come back till Monday, so we should be safe if we leave at half-past," Irene replied.

"That sounds like a plan. Let's do it," said Grace.

Irene was tanned from her swimming holiday in Italy during the summer, and she was looking forward to showing off her arms in a fancy dress. She wondered where the little black dress was, that she wore to her father's recent retirement party, and did she get it back from the dry cleaner's last time she sent it there.

She had really enjoyed the holiday with Gary, they had gone for five days, and she swam in the Mediterranean for what seemed like hours at a time and then they would play tennis together. They stayed in a friend's villa, and it was the second year of their invitation.

Gary was certainly envious of his friend's good fortune, that he could own a villa and wondered if he would ever be able to do the same. For now, he was

Chapter 2

just enjoying Irene's company and the holiday was low key and incredibly special.

Grace, pretty and larger-framed, was a little younger than Irene. She'd been working in accounts for three months following a successful apprenticeship when Irene started working there as a secretary to the partners. That was two years ago. They became firm friends and shared all their gripes about the office over their frequent coffees and occasional pots of tea.

Grace wasn't in a relationship herself, but occasionally she dated and was happy that Irene had found Gary early on after beginning online dating. As anyone who had been through this could tell you, it could potentially be a minefield.

Gary and Irene were usually together when Irene wasn't working out and Gary wasn't at the tennis club. This didn't seem to bother Grace, although occasionally there was a feeling that three was a crowd. Gary monopolised Irene.

"He just worries about me," said Irene, when Grace brought it up, knowing he was worrying about her food issues, which were a non-issue as far as Irene was concerned.

She insisted on eating a gluten-free diet as much as possible. Although she was not coeliac, she was afraid of bloat and generally had a problem showing how lovely she naturally looked. All the swimming and working out in the world and food obsession wouldn't change that.

Just then, Suzanne Barron came by, and Irene and Grace had to stop talking. She was the boss, after all, and Suzanne didn't like unnecessary chat.

Suzanne was wearing a navy suit and was carrying paperwork in her hands as she stepped into the coffee station.

"Are you having a nice break?" she said to Irene. The tone was possibly sarcastic, Irene wasn't sure, but she noticed it, nonetheless.

"Be a dear and do two sets of these for me when you finish."

"Sure Suzanne. When do you want them done by?" Irene said matter-of-factly, and annoyed that she still had to do photocopying. She was also not too pleased about being called dear.

To Irene, all the documents should be online. As a younger staff member, she didn't understand the older partner's obsession with paper copies of everything.

Suzanne must have been presenting a proposal to them. In any case, why couldn't she use her own photocopier?

By lunchtime is fine.

"No problem," said Irene, biting her tongue.

Suzanne Barron was a managing partner at the firm where they all worked, and she oversaw both the accounts' function and administration. So, both Grace and Irene reported to her.

Slim, with a sleek blonde bob hairstyle, Suzanne was a little older than the others, maybe forty at a push. She too, played at the same club where Gary played tennis. Irene guessed she would probably be at the party on Saturday.

Grace and Irene finished their coffee and said no more about the plan for Friday just then. Later, there was a slight paper jam with the photocopying, and Irene cursed silently, but still she got it done.

She was looking forward to a Friday shopping expedition and making a splash at the party.

Suzanne usually took a late lunch and then worked into the evening so there was rarely an opportunity for Irene to sneak off for a wash and blow-dry or a spot of shopping on a flexible schedule and make it up afterwards. The partners didn't like that type of shoddy timekeeping anyway, so it probably wouldn't have been possible. They didn't believe in flexible timekeeping, working from home, or any of that new-fangled nonsense.

Irene normally went swimming after work, it cleared her head of any annoying or irritating thoughts of the day's activities, and it kept her mentally and physically in top condition, ready for the evening ahead and the next morning.

She enjoyed clearing her mind of any stray intrusive thoughts. She practised mindfulness with a calming application through her social media account.

Tuesdays and Thursdays Irene and Grace felt safe to leave directly on time, but the other nights they had to stay right to the end of the day because Suzanne always wanted more spreadsheets done, or urgent help with presentations.

Chapter 2

It seemed like in this business, you had to keep chasing your tail to get out of the rat race, and you had to work from eight in the morning until six at night just to keep your position at the firm, never mind get promoted. It appeared to Irene that she was helping Suzanne get up in the partners' goods books, but that she didn't get any credit for staying late and doing any extra.

But for the partners, Irene guessed they were always busy. She didn't have to take work related calls at home, at least not at this stage in her career. She certainly didn't carry a mobile phone from work which would have made her constantly contactable. Which is something Suzanne had to do.

On Thursday afternoon, Suzanne spoke to Irene.

"I need to you to do some research for me, she said. "Anything you can find out about the new Kouba buildings. Kouba is a suburb south-east of the central city of Algiers in northern Algeria. I have a late meeting tomorrow and I want to do some risk management about our investments there."

"Tomorrow?" said Irene, crestfallen. "You mean Friday?"

"Yes of course I mean Friday. You can look up the deal on the website that we launched recently. Here's the website address," she said, handing Irene a piece of paper.

"That's fine. I'll do my best," said Irene, disappointed.

"And I'll be doing a presentation, so I'll need it first thing in the morning".

"Of course, I'll do it," said Irene, and stole a quick glance at Grace, who had her head stuck in a spreadsheet at her workstation during the conversation.

It looked like they wouldn't get their early day off after all.

The following morning Irene did the research and presented it to Suzanne.

"Good work," Suzanne said. "Now I can do the presentation and be out of here by two o'clock. Can you manage the office?"

"Of course, Suzanne. But didn't you say that you had a meeting?" asked Irene, a little puzzled.

"It's an off-site meeting," Suzanne said brusquely.

"Well, good luck."

Just as she had given up on her shopping trip, it looked like Irene and Grace might be able to make it after all. The new clerk at the reception desk would manage all the calls and take over if needed.

She felt a bit guilty leaving the office, but she really did want to look good for the party at the tennis club. She had trained in the pool for weeks and ate only soup for lunch for ages!

Perhaps she didn't have her priorities quite right, but this just wasn't the time to think about it now, for Irene anyway.

Two o'clock soon came around, and Suzanne left with her laptop on cue. Taking a quick glance around her desk, Irene verified that she had taken her bag and mobile phone with her. Her plan for an early afternoon was working. It most certainly looked like Suzanne had left for the weekend and would not be returning.

Chapter 3

By two-thirty Irene and Grace figured the coast was clear and powered down their computers to leave for the afternoon. Irene popped her head into the senior partner's office and asked if anyone needed her or Grace for the afternoon, as Suzanne had left, and they wanted to go early. The partner said they weren't needed so long as the front desk was covered.

Happy days! Irene and Grace had their time-in-lieu sheets filled out and left on their desks if any questions were asked by Suzanne when they returned on Monday.

"See you Monday," said Grace. "Have fun!"

"I will, thanks. See you soon," said Irene.

She knew the new dress shop on the corner had a gorgeous black crushed velvet dress, and she was keeping her fingers crossed they would have it in her size. If not, she could always go to the other boutique on the high street to pick up something.

They always had good, natty little outfits at this time of year, just in time for the party season, or something nice left over from the summer sales.

She had looked for the black dress she'd worn to her dad's party, and she realised she didn't have it anymore. Perhaps she gave it to a charity shop, or she may have sold it in her last set of consignment gear when she was clearing out her wardrobe.

Irene left the building and went to the store on the corner of Oxford Street. She was lucky on two counts. She found the black dress in her size and tried it on. It looked perfect. She then found the most elegant pair of shoes to top the outfit off. Gary would be pleased, she thought.

She found she had lots of time and arrived home at four o'clock. Throwing her coat on a hanger, she came into the kitchen and put on the kettle. She noticed Gary's coat on the chair in the living room and thought he must be upstairs changing. She wondered what he'd be doing at home this time on a Friday, but she was pleased, nonetheless.

"I'll surprise him," she said to herself.

She waited for the kettle to boil and made two cups of tea and brought them upstairs.

He would never expect her to be home from work. It would be a nice surprise.

"Maybe we'll make love," she thought. She remembered the kiss he gave her that morning when he handed her toast for breakfast, the tender caress on her bare shoulders before she dressed for work.

It was only for a moment that she thought about these things, and then put them to the back of her mind.

He might not be in the mood. He's been a little distracted lately, she thought.

Irene entered the bedroom quietly, and she noticed the crumpled duvet on the floor.

Suddenly got the shock of her life and nearly dropped the teacups to the floor and then she shrieked.

Suzanne and Gary were on the bed, wearing only underwear! Gary had boxer shorts on, and Suzanne was wearing a lacy bra and French knicker set.

The penny finally dropped for poor Irene.

Gary's face flushed, and he didn't say anything at first, but struggled to get his tee-shirt back on in a hurry, and then spoke.

"Honey, I can explain! Honestly, I can."

"Forget explanations Gary, said Suzanne. What are you doing here now? You should be at work!"

Chapter 3

Irene suddenly saw red and exploded.

"You're joking right? You're crazy, Suzanne! You're talking to me about work? When you're sleeping with Gary?"

She paused.

"Don't think this is over Suzanne. And you, Gary, how could you do this to me? We're together for two years, for God's sake. What about our future? Don't you care about that?"

At twenty-five years old, and in her first serious relationship, Irene was young enough to think that all relationships remained meant to last.

She didn't know what the future held for her, but she didn't know what to do either now.

Suddenly, she felt trapped.

"It's not what it looks like," Gary said, suddenly concerned.

Suzanne chimed in apparently oblivious to the effect this was having on Irene.

"It's exactly what it looks like, Gary; tell her, for all our sakes!"

"That's not for you to say, Suzanne and you're not helping," retorted Gary.

Gary was trying to cover his tracks now that he had two women in the same room and his cover seemed to be blown.

"Just go. Just go, Suzanne," he continued. I'll talk to you more about the deal in the morning. You won't get away with freezing me out."

He nodded to Suzanne and motioned her out of the room.

Gary paused and put on his tee-shirt.

"Did you hear what I just said? Just put on some clothes and get out," Gary shouted to Suzanne when she did not move.

Suzanne muttered something under her breath to Gary, (possibly a swear word), then she grabbed her clothes and stomped out of the bedroom. Suzanne left the apartment suddenly without further ado.

"What is this deal?" asked Irene after a pause.

She had been shaking so hard with anger her face was red and sweating.

She didn't wait for Gary to reply. She spoke again.

"What are you doing - this business deal with Suzanne?

"Oh Irene, it's better you don't know. That's the truth."

"I demand to know! How long has it been going on? Is that why you're sleeping with her? Because you are doing some deal? Is she the only one you're sleeping with? Are there others? Does our relationship mean nothing to you?"

Irene felt like her world was about to implode.

"I'll explain if you'll listen."

Irene was having none of it.

"Please, Irene, please let me explain."

The irony of Irene only finding out about the betrayal by Gary because she had skipped out on her boss was not lost on her.

But it didn't stop her being furious.

What excuse could he come up with to get himself out of this scenario?

Gary thought for a few minutes before he responded.

He had always thought he was happy with Irene. In fact, he was delighted when they moved in together after such a short time.

She was so attractive and pretty, he thought he was the luckiest man alive. He didn't know what to think anymore. He just knew that he wasn't happy now, and recently he has been acting out, and hurting people he cared about.

However, he'd always had a roving eye, and he was weak and flawed like many in his family. His father, for one, who mistreated his mother.

He never thought he would end up treating anyone badly, but he was treating Irene badly. Whatever scenario he got into with Suzanne, it wasn't just about the drama.

The fact of it was, he didn't know what he wanted and that's the truth.

He was devoted to his daughter Rosie though, and he was devastated when things didn't work out with her mother, Julia.

He would be heartbroken if anything happened to the relationship with Rosie. She had been a light in his life through very dark days a few years ago, and he wondered if he was going through dark days again. Or if they could get darker.

He now remembered how others said had been spoiled as a child and had everything come to him so easily. Some people thought that in one sense he had rebelled, and maybe that was true.

Chapter 3

But none of this mattered now.

Irene was irate that he had cheated on her after he swore blind that he would never betray her like that.

And Gary realised that because of his foolishness his relationship with Irene was breaking down, just like it had with Julia before.

Soon they would have to uncouple their living arrangements, just the same as with Rosie's mother. Would he ever learn?

Damn Suzanne anyway.

Could things get any worse for Gary?

Chapter 4

On the morning of the same day, in a London police station, Constable Rodney Mooney was working on a computer. He scratched his chin as the computer flagged a suspicious email account coming in from an outside server. Rodney was curious.

This didn't happen very often, but when it did it was suspicious. Even though Constable Mooney was no computer expert, he was able to access the email remotely using the skills he had learned on a course to do with cyber-security and and he was able to decrypt the message.

First, he needed to make sure there was no executable file attached to the message before he opened it. Then he passed it through a piece of software he had on his computer to decrypt the characters and words of the message. *South Dock 15.55, 4/3* he reckoned was the code. He mentally made a note of what he learned and put a written memo into his notebook, for filing later.

Even paper notebooks had their uses.

Rodney had just received a tip-off from one of his colleagues that there was a major drug bust that he needed to be at. Rodney thought this could have a connection to the email from the outside server. He wanted to wait for more information, but because the Chief Inspector made the request, he had to go at once.

"Come on, let us go for a late lunch and a coffee first, before we make this arrest," Rodney's colleague Sergeant Moran said, ignoring the immediacy.

Chapter 4

"It should be a doddle. The guys got no priors."

"Right you are, Sergeant."

The two men prepared to leave the station. They packed up their things from the worktop from where they had been working on the police computer.

Rodney and Moran had just discussed the man who *did have* a prior record.

"So do you think he is a thief as well as a drug dealer?" said Rodney.

"We are not sure but it's certainly looking that way," said the Sergeant. "This guy has priors for serious incidents - and we do know that the drug dealing is definite," according to what I have been told.

"Are you saying that the drug dealing? The drug stash that we found at the docks in the shipping container the other week - are you saying that's related to this guy that we need to see now?" asked Rodney.

"That's exactly what I'm saying. We need to get behind this quickly and ensure that it's an easy win for the Metropolitan."

"Shipping containers holding this level of drug activity usually come tied with a major criminal element besides that, and I'm not sure yet exactly what the full story is, but I've got enough to arrest this guy and search his apartment."

"Right Sarge," said Rodney. "Should we go and have our lunch now?"

"The inspector wants us to go and sort this out but sure yeah, let's go and have lunch. It can't hurt to fill our stomachs before we go out - you never know what's going to happen on a job."

"Besides, there's a curry chips or a steak and kidney pie with my name on it in the canteen."

Rodney and the Sergeant stopped off in the canteen on the second floor as they had been in early and had worked up an appetite. It was three o'clock. Famished, it seemed a pie and chip dinner with a pot of coffee would be just the ticket.

Just then the chief superintendent came by and spoke to the men.

"The wrong body was in the casket of that Epping Funeral Parlour. We've got to investigate. Sergeant, I need you to work on that internal investigation audit matter."

The sergeant put down his fork and spoke.

"But chief we must do this drug recovery and arrest on a license in the city. Trust me, you will need to know exactly what's going on. And it could be linked to problems we have been having all over London. Are you sure it cannot wait? The Inspector has an urgent matter we need to deal with."

"Well, it can," said the chief. "But only until the end of the day, What's with the pie and chips then if you're in such a rush?"

"We missed lunch!"

Just then, the Inspector came into the canteen holding stab vests.

"C'mon lads, he said, you really must go to that stash house in an apartment complex in the city. The one I was telling you about, near the docklands."

"OK," said the Chief, "you're off the hook with the funeral parlour job. For now!"

"Thanks Chief," replied the Inspector. To the two men still seated at the table, he said "It should be an easy enough matter but look sharpish," the Inspector said "And put on your proper gear, that uniform will not do the way it is. You do not look that great Sergeant. The guy we need to arrest is a lawyer, so we must do everything by the book, not that we wouldn't anyway! But I really want to throw the key away on him, because law professionals really should know better than this type of crime!"

"So, does this guy have any earlier form for this? Does he have any priors? Or is he squeaky clean?"

"Not much, just a few parking tickets. No drugs."

"And what's the plan of action for this arrest?"

"Do we have a warrant or is it just a fishing expedition?"

"What's the connection to the other case we're working on?"

"Is there a cyber-crime element?"

"I know we've got computer records of his, but is that all there is?"

"Will he wriggle out of it?"

"There are drugs."

"I know there are, boss. But can we tie him to them?"

"There's a real dodgy set up in that apartment. I can feel it in my bones."

"I can't quite put my finger on it."

"There's something going on."

Chapter 4

"Come on let's go. We can have our pie and chips later."

The older man, Sergeant Moran, grabbed a Snickers bar from the counter and put it into his pocket with the coffee to go in his other hand.

He sighed.

It could be a long evening, what with the Chief's internal audit work needing to be done when he gets back from work in the field.

Constable Rodney Mooney, the younger man, grabbed his paper notebook and phone and put it into the front pocket of his uniform jacket.

The two men left the station building, not really knowing what would await them. Like any day, having a plan of action for any eventuality is one of the jobs of the police.

Chapter 5

On the other side of London from down by the docks, just after Suzanne had left the apartment, while Irene and Gary were still talking, suddenly, there was a knock on the door at the apartment. There was the sound of *thud-thud* of hard knuckles rapping on the door and the racket of a couple of people outside.

Whoever they were they must have gotten access to the apartment building by the front door past the concierge, and now all that was between Irene and Gary and whoever it was, was the apartment door, which wasn't all that thick or sturdy.

Gary was none too pleased. He made a mental note to reprimand Joe, the concierge, for not alerting him to visitors.

Of all the times for a caller, now was not one of them.

"Go away. It's not a good time," Gary called out.

"Gary Russell? Are you in there? It's the police," called the Sergeant through the closed door. He motioned to his colleague to move closer to the door and prepare to break it down if necessary.

"Come out, come out now. We're looking for Gary Russell. We know this is your apartment, and we're not going away until we speak to you."

Gary was motionless and frozen to the spot. He didn't know what to say, but he knew he had to think quickly.

There was so much going on with him right now, the last thing he wanted

Chapter 5

was a visit from the cops!

Not only had he been in the middle of a blazing row with his partner, and he'd just been caught with his pants down, literally. It was just minutes after Irene had come home and found him in bed with Suzanne. Really, it wasn't a good time. Gary was thinking a mile a minute as the next few years of his life lay before him like a black cloud.

Feeling guilty about being caught out with Suzanne, he had just admitted to a business arrangement to Irene that he'd taken part in with Suzanne. He couldn't be sure he could rely on Irene to keep quiet on the matter, or Suzanne for that matter, not if the police were involved.

It wasn't his fault really, he had gambling debts and an ex-partner and daughter who had a need for lifestyle funding. Oh, and there was the small matter of a minor drug habit, 'well it wasn't really a habit, it was just recreational,' he told himself.

But there must be some reason the police were there. They don't call randomly to people's apartments and demand to gain entry, do they? It was all a good deal of trouble for him.

And the business with Suzanne wasn't really a business arrangement. Would that come out with the police? He really hoped not. Suzanne had suggested it to him.

It wasn't him, was it? He wasn't dishonest, was he? He just took a financial kickback on a couple of loans. Didn't he? How much? £200,000 pounds in Cryptocurrency. That was quite a lot of money even in London. For each of the parties to the transaction. Yes, each. But he didn't have access to the money, he thought. It was taken away unbeknownst to him. It was a gambling problem. Yes, that's right a gambling problem. Everyone did that kind of thing in London. It's part of the underworld, isn't it? Did they do that kind of thing? In London, or anywhere else? Didn't they? He didn't really know. Not so much. White collar crime? Not blue collar. Isn't that what they call it these days.

There it was, it wasn't the right thing to do, Gary knew that and now the police had come knocking on their door. He didn't expect that today.

Not today, this Friday evening, he hadn't expected to be caught out by Irene firstly over Suzanne, and certainly not by the police. It was his first time doing anything dishonest, as far as he knew, and the guilt was written all over him. He knew as a lawyer that the police could sniff guilt a mile off.

What was a man to do?

He and Suzanne got involved in the deception, they were jointly or separately responsible, and the crime, if that's what it was, was over and done with now.

Loyal Irene. Or was she so loyal? Would she stand by him, and did he care anyway? What was he thinking, of course he cared.

Certainly, he needed her, and wanted her, but his mind was changing so much that he really didn't know what to think. His neck was sweating now under his shirt collar that he had hastily put on while Irene was getting ready to open the door.

She would never forgive him. That was the least of his worries.

But he wasn't thinking about Irene now.

Really, he was only thinking about himself. And trying to get himself out of this sorry mess, whatever that was going to turn out to be.

Damn straight she wouldn't forgive him.

Is it possible he underestimated her?

She certainly showed a side to herself he hadn't seen before today.

A feisty lady.

"Come on out, Gary, I know you're in there. We can hear you! We know you've been having a row with someone, and you need to come out. Now! We're going to break the door down if you're not out in ten seconds' flat."

The temperate, loyal Irene was silent during this time, although she had been fiery and flaming angry just moments earlier.

She finally left the bedroom, downstairs, and into the hall of their apartment towards the front entrance.

"I'll let you in, one second!" she said to the police officers outside the door, and then to Gary she said, "We're going to have to let the police in and I don't know what they want but put the rest of your clothes on for pity's sake. Nobody wants to see your bare legs!"

When the door was open, and the police arrived through it, there were two men in uniform facing Irene and Gary.

Chapter 5

A younger police constable, and his detective Sergeant.

The two men from the police station who had been missing their pie and chips, Constable Rodney, and Sergeant Moran.

The younger one of the officers was no more than Irene's age, maybe twenty-five. He was tall and clean-shaven and had a baton. He was accompanied by a man who was older, maybe forty-five years old. He was gray-haired and a little shorter.

"What can I do for you officers?" said Gary, cool as ice, but trembling inside as he never thought this day would come. "What brings you to my private residence? Knocking down the door in the middle of the afternoon!

I'm in my underwear in case you hadn't noticed."

"Yes, we know," replied one of the officers. "You can get dressed in a minute but enough of the impertinence, Mr. Russell."

"We suspect you're involved in drug smuggling, and we have arrest warrants here and we're allowed to search your apartment," said Sergeant Moran, matter-of-factly.

Gary really hadn't been expecting this. His face went white, and the entire colour drained from his cheeks ghost-like.

The two police officers were none too happy to see Gary impolite and barely decent. But they could see he was shocked to see them, and that they had the element of surprise. Perhaps they would get back to the station for their pie and chips after all. This was what they needed on a Friday afternoon. An easy job. They could soon be enjoying their pie and chips back at the station in the officers' mess hall.

"Okay, what is this about? Officers? Please. I haven't done anything wrong. I'm a lawyer. There must be some mistake!" Pleaded Gary.

"You're wanted for questioning in relation to drug smuggling and fraud. Come away with us now, or it will be worse for you," the Sergeant continued. "Our warrant to search the apartment is on suspicion of drug smuggling contrary to common law. We are monitoring your bank accounts and we need you to provide access to your computer equipment and phones."

Irene stood motionless and quiet. She could scarcely believe her ears.

Gary angrily led them through the kitchen and showed them the medicine cabinet where there was nothing more sinister than diet pills, protein shakes and paracetamol.

The stash of tablets he had hidden was in a locker at the tennis club, and it was for private use, he told himself. He thought he was hiding the habit, but Suzanne knew about it anyway. That's how she got him involved in the matter, as she had a contact who sold it to him so they couldn't be traced.

His partner Irene didn't know about it, of course either, for as much as she knew Gary during their two years together, she was now coming to realise she didn't really know him at all.

She foolishly thought their life was just dandy! She never suspected he would do drugs - he didn't even smoke cigarettes, but that's exactly what he wanted her to think.

Irene and Gary both assumed that the arrest and search of their home must be some mistake, as Gary never thought he would be caught, and Irene genuinely didn't know what had been going on until that point.

Irene mistakenly thought that the police arrived at the door because some of the neighbours complained about their rowing, or Gary and Suzanne's afternoon delight in the bedroom, but that was unlikely.

It was a London suburb, weren't there always people rowing?

Gary knew it was serious though, and before too long he was hauled away in handcuffs in the back of the squad car and driven to a police station by the London Metropolitan police, and Irene was left in the apartment wondering what to do. Was she capable of going on for now?

She really didn't know what was going on with her and Gary, or him and Suzanne for that matter. There were so many questions left unanswered.

She wasn't going to put up with unfaithfulness or any court trial that Gary might be involved in. No, she certainly wasn't.

Was she?

Maybe she would wait until later to decide that, but for now she couldn't bear the thought of supporting him.

Financially, emotionally, or any other way.

They had been together for two years, but what a roller coaster ride, she thought. Now Gary was arrested, he was a person of interest in drug smuggling, and he could well be indicated in a fraud investigation.

Not to mention he was cheating on her; how could she possibly stay with him after that?

And could she stay out of jail herself if she was implicated and accused wrongly? Her thoughts went spinning out of control and she soon had a headache.

She knew how these things could happen and escalate, she had seen it happen in news stories and in the media. If there was anything that she was implicated in, she could be found to have been too stupid to know about it and if there was money about, she could be accused of receiving it, and then well - she could have trouble calling knocking on her door.

Chapter 6

Irene swore to herself that if Gary had engaged in drug smuggling, she'd kill him! But he'd be locked up so she wouldn't have to and that would be a good thing. So many questions.

They hauled Gary away in handcuffs and all the while he insisted there must be some mistake.

Suzanne was probably destroying evidence as it looked like she may get away scott-free. She hadn't been implicated yet, but that was only as far as Irene knew, she didn't know the full story after all.

She wasn't in the apartment at the time. But maybe the police would know where she lived too.

Suzanne must know what's going on because it's got her name all over it, this arrest warrant, Irene thought.

If Gary's implicated in anything it's down to Suzanne, she was sure of it. Yet she wasn't sure of anything. She had a sick feeling in her stomach as her anxiety levels soared and her headache was getting worse.

"Commercial Real Estate partner indeed! There's more to that lady than meets the eye!" thought Irene about her boss.

Obviously, Gary wasn't stupid. He was not admitting to anything, but Irene wondered about the cryptic clue he mentioned in the bedroom with Suzanne, implying that there was some business deal they taken part in together.

What was it? They hadn't mentioned the specifics, but it must be serious to have the London Metropolitan Police come knocking.

Could this be the deal they were talking about? Irene had no evidence to draw a conclusion of any kind, but her suspicion was that Suzanne was the manipulator and Gary was just plain weak.

"Whatever is going on, it's got to be down to Suzanne," she thought.

Down at the police station, Gary was taken to an interview room and questioned under caution about his involvement in drug smuggling.

Gary said he had nothing to say and knew nothing about it. He had no idea what was going on.

"I need legal representation for any further questions," he said. "I have the right to refuse to answer any questions."

"Now, Mr. Russell, there's no need for that," said the constable.

Gary replied, "no comment", to every question put to him.

This worsened the situation no end and annoyed the officers questioning him.

Detective Constable Rodney finally spoke.

"Yes Mr. Russell, you have the right to remain silent. You can lawyer up, that's for sure. It may do you no good in court, but it'll do me good. One word from me and the Chief will lock you up without a bail order, and then the judge will throw away the key once you're found guilty."

He pauses for effect.

"However, if you cooperate you might make it off lightly, we don't know for sure. The evidence is pointing to you although we're waiting to hear back from the squad team about the stash we found at the airport, and we will get to the bottom of that. We absolutely will, Gary. Make no mistake."

Gary didn't know what to say, but he continued listening.

"You make sure that you've got all your alibis lined up because we're going to go to the end of the earth, to make sure the right person goes down for these drugs. Don't forget there was a customs officer injured on duty. Not to mention the fraud that we suspect you to be involved in. The drugs, they need to be off the streets, Gary. They ruin people's lives!"

The Constable paused again.

He wanted to make sure the good cop, bad cop routine was working, and that he had the best chance of breaking Gary into confessing and telling them what they wanted him to say.

"Have you anything else to say?"

"Just that I've never done drugs in my life, Constable, I don't even smoke a cigarette. I don't do anything wrong!"

Gary nearly believed it himself. Not quite, but nearly.

It was true though; he didn't do *major* street drugs. Just the ecstasy tablets that Suzanne's friend had sorted him out with. And the cannabis he had tried in his university days. He honestly never thought this day would come.

Gary pleaded with Constable Rodney to let him go and stop the interview.

He didn't know what to do, and he didn't have a lawyer present by this time either.

But soon, his legal counsel arrived, a man named Neil Skater, the same age as Gary, thirty-five years old, but stouter and balder, bounded into the interview room.

"What's going on here?" Neil Skater said. He had a booming voice that filled the small room. "This man has been charged with a serious crime, and his rights have been violated."

"I'm just doing my job," Constable Rodney said. "I'm not here to defend myself against your allegations. You're the lawyer. Defend him if you can."

"I'm going to," Neil said. "Now what is my client being charged with."

"It's the first step in the investigation, but we suspect him of drug smuggling and fraud," replied the Constable.

"That's not true," Gary said. "I didn't do anything."

"You think you can deny everything," Constable Rodney said. "We're trying to get at the truth before we bring you to court."

The police officer and Neil Skater had a stare down. The two men were about the same height, over six feet, and both had plenty of physical presence.

"I'm going to talk to my client alone," Neil Skater said. "In private."

"Then I will be outside," Constable Rodney said. "In case you need to talk to me." He stared again at Neil Skater for a moment and then left the room.

Gary's lawyer sat down in front of him, and Gary's hands shook uncontrol-

Chapter 6

lably. Neil Skater put his hand on Gary's shoulder and leaned forward.

"Relax, Gary," Neil said quietly, and then turned around and sat on the spare chair in the interview room. The room was badly lit, a little damp and had navy blue paint on the lower half of the walls, with yellow on the upper half. The chair was cold, hard, and uncomfortable to sit in.

Gary told his lawyer that he had nothing to do with drugs smuggling, and what the police thought they knew must be a mistake.

"Relax, Gary," Neil said quietly. "I talked to the prosecutor. They don't have anything on you. This is just a formality."

Gary tried to believe him, but he couldn't. The anxiety he now felt was like a weight on his chest, and he felt nauseous and sick.

Gary never mentioned the deception with Suzanne that was constantly on his mind since he was roped into Suzanne's property scheme a few months ago. He didn't know what to say or what to do about it.

"What happened at the arrest?" Neil asked. "Is this the first time you've met that officer?"

"I never met him before," confirmed Gary.

"Well, they don't have anything on you. They can't take you to trial. The state has to drop the charges."

Gary's eyes teared up, and he looked down at his hands as they trembled. He couldn't believe what was happening. The last few months of his life had been ruined by a stupid affair gone bad.

It didn't matter that Suzanne was the one who ordered the drug-smuggling operation that led to the injury of the customs agent, and it didn't matter that he barely knew about the matter at hand. The fact that he used to work with Suzanne was enough for them to pin the smuggling on him.

He didn't want to mention the deception with Suzanne that was constantly on his mind since he was roped into Suzanne's scheme a few months ago. The white-collar crime. The Cryptocurrency received. Surely there were no consequences of that. The loans with no security. For planning applications. For properties that may or may not exist now or in the future. No harm done if the loan was being serviced by payments. Just a small kick back of a few quid wouldn't hurt anyone. How many pounds? Two hundred thousand pounds? In crypto? Each? Not enough to go to jail.

Not nearly. Not half.

The interview started again, and Mr. Skater tried to persuade the constable that he should let his client go, pending further investigation.

The constable reluctantly agreed to suspend the interview pending further investigation, but he would not allow him to get police bail. He wasn't told he could go. In fact, he was remanded in custody.

"You're on my radar, Mr. Russell. Just watch yourself," he concluded.

Gary didn't say anything further. Terrified, he just waited until he was told he could go.

"We will be watching you inside and investigating very thoroughly."

Gary was still silent.

"If you had any accomplices, this is the time to tell me, Gary. It's time to give them up," the constable said, "Anyone at all that you should not be associated with, anybody who's taking drugs, doing drugs, smuggling drugs, laundering money, or anything like that at all. Or anything else. You should co-operate and tell me now. It'll be better for you in the long run."

The Constable asked Gary if there was any statement he wanted to make at this time.

"No comment," said Gary.

Gary was terrified by now and wiped his brow which was now covered with sweat.

A sweaty brow was never a good look, he thought, and not in a police station, remanded in custody!

Chapter 7

On opposite ends of the London Underground line that they usually travelled, Gary and Irene were now spending time apart from each other. A forced separation, but a separation, nonetheless.

Gary was incarcerated in the police station awaiting charging.

Irene was at home.

Friday night at Irene and Gary's house was usually pizza night. Occasionally, they had a Chinese takeaway, but usually pizza.

Gluten-free for Irene because of her strict swimming schedule and her unfounded fear that she would somehow look bloated in her costume. It wasn't true. She was on the local swimming team for years since she was a girl in school, and then again, in college, and now although she didn't swim competitively anymore, it was the most relaxing thing she found she could do in times of great anxiety.

Gary played tennis at a local club, so he was careful too, but on Friday they had been accustomed to a treat: a date night with a takeaway and a bottle of wine to share all their conversations about how the week had gone and do a little bit of couple's bonding.

Despite everything, they didn't go out too often, for all their appearance of supposedly financially rewarding careers.

Now, even with Gary's involvement in what appeared to be a significant fraud, they still had moderate tastes and knew how to manage money.

But maybe that was all a front.

Irene began to think. Maybe Gary was lying all along, and he was lining his own pockets for some other reason. Maybe it was more about Suzanne than he thought.

Maybe he was thinking about Rosie and Julia again and wanted to provide more for them. Or maybe he really did care about Suzanne. Maybe he really cared for her, and it wasn't all about the money.

Right up until tonight, Irene would have been sure about him. That he was loyal to her and their shared future that she had planned. She thought they both wanted the same things.

But then, maybe that wasn't the only thing going on. Irene may have had other plans all along too, maybe she was too young and the age difference between them really mattered. This was her first serious relationship, and she had high hopes for it.

Thinking that she could have it all, she idolized Gary to an extent.

Now it was Friday night and Irene was sitting alone in the apartment thinking. Will I go to my mum and dad's house? No, they'll be too judgmental. Will I go out with my friends? No, they'll be too judgmental. Will I stay home? No, too lonely. Just me and my thoughts. Maybe I will go to the gym. Yes, that's it. I'll go to the gym.

In the end Irene went swimming. She didn't have pizza or wine that night.

She waited for Gary to call because she was not going to the police station to bail him out. But then she remembered, he didn't get station bail, he was still incarcerated because the charges were so serious, and perhaps he was still being questioned.

She was so livid with him; she didn't want to wait for him to be released. She wasn't so sure she wanted him at home tonight anyway.

Besides, she was available on the mobile anyway if he rang, and she would only be in the swimming pool for an hour.

She arrived at the pool and changed into her black two-piece swimming costume and showered and put on her latex cap.

Going into the chlorinated pool area to swim her usual twenty lengths, she noticed the younger police officer who had earlier arrested Gary at their apartment standing on the edge of the pool on the far side. He appeared to

Chapter 7

be giving private swimming lessons to teenagers.

According to the name tag on his tank-top his name was Rodney. She didn't remember if he mentioned his name earlier during the time of the arrest, she was so upset at the time with what happened with Gary.

Suits him, Irene thought.

He was just as tall as she remembered, and now she could see the full length of his maleness in his shorts, tank-top and flip-flops.

Must be his time off, she thought, and wondered if police officers got paid so poorly that they had to take second jobs. Or did he just like swimming as much as she did?

She never suspected it was a community diversion programme to help at-risk kids stay away from crime, and they were organising a swimming gala to keep the kids off the street.

She never suspected he could once have been one of those teenagers, and he had been inspired by a police officer he had met as a youngster to join the force and become a trainee officer.

She never suspected he had a younger brother with autism who he had to take care of sometimes, and that was one of the reasons he missed school when he was younger, graduating, without major qualifications.

Rodney was a world apart from Gary, the tennis club going, public schooled man-child, who won her over with his easy charm and wit.

And who was now embroiled in some major scandal which might cause her problems with her family, her career, and her privacy.

Damn Gary, anyway.

She didn't know anything about Rodney.

In fact, she hadn't met him. Yet.

When Gary finally called on the telephone, she was on the underground on the way home from the pool.

"I can't talk, Gary. I'm on the train. In fact, I don't want to talk to you anyway," she said, and she hung up.

There, see if he can cheat on me and get away with it, thought Irene. I wonder what he wanted. Is he coming home? Does he need bail? There's so much we need to talk about. Maybe there isn't that much talking to be done. How could he do this to me anyway?

As she left the train, Irene felt a pang of hunger and decided to treat herself on the way home.

On the west side of Irene's apartment building was a café where she occasionally got a smoothie with peanut butter, and since she had preferred to skip dinner that night, she stopped in for a takeaway treat.

As you do when your partner's in jail, of course, the only thing you can do is go to the pool and the smoothie bar.

It appears the detective constable from earlier, Rodney, had the same idea and showed up at the smoothie bar too, his hair ruffled and still a little damp. Or maybe he was following her. Maybe he had her under surveillance and was under the orders of the Chief or the Superintendent.

She didn't know. She didn't know anything about Rodney. She didn't know anything more about Gary and she thought she knew him for years. They shared a house and a relationship, and after all, she thought she had a future with him. Not that she wanted to appear fickle or anything, but now she didn't know what to think. Yes, best to swim it off, and clear her head entirely just for the few moments that she could swim lengths and forget about all the worries in the world. She was calm after her swim.

Rodney suddenly sidled over to where Irene was sitting and asked to sit there too.

"Is this seat taken?" said Rodney to Irene, just as she was about to put her straw into the smoothie.

"No, it's not taken," said Irene. "But we shouldn't talk - unless it's official."

"Do we need to talk officially?" said Rodney.

"I'm just here for a snack, as I missed dinner - going swimming - and I suspect you know that. Didn't you see me at the pool?"

"Oh, were you at the pool? I was too busy with my young teenage charges to notice. I teach swimming two nights a week to youngsters from the local area. I would have said hello if I had noticed you. Didn't we meet earlier somewhere?"

"No, we didn't," said Irene. "We didn't meet. You just barged into my apartment earlier today. It must be a lousy job you have if you get your kicks

Chapter 7

out of barging into people's homes when they're in their underwear and having domestic arguments."

"It's exceedingly difficult," said Rodney, quietly. "We don't like going into people's houses any more than they like having us come in. But sometimes it's useful to have a police officer on your side if you're in trouble for instance, usually they can help."

"But today? I shouldn't be talking to you about this." Irene looked like she had something to get off her chest.

"Yes?" continued Rodney, suddenly curious. "Go on."

Irene paused. "I really don't know that much about my partner's business, but if there's anything I can help with, I'll assist you if I can."

"That's helpful. Thanks, we'll be in touch when we need to talk to you, and it might be sooner rather than later. It's Irene, isn't it? I'm Rodney, and here is my card." He handed her a business card with his name and office address details on it and she quickly put it in her pocket.

With that, Irene took her take-away drink to her apartment at the building next door, as she didn't want to stay hanging around talking to Rodney any further. He might be good looking, but she was wary of him, and she didn't know him.

When she went to sleep that night, she woke up with a headache and went into work sometime later than planned.

The previous day's events were behind her.

The next time she noticed Rodney at the swimming pool he was coming out of the building, and he was wearing his policeman's uniform. This time she noticed the community members with him as they were young charges in the pool because he had been instructing them to swim.

She noticed his blue eyes and the respectful way he glanced at her, appearing to appreciate her, yet saying nothing at all.

It was somehow proper.

She thought this, in the context of how they met that is, but not in the context of how she might want him to make her feel in the future.

She was beginning to have feelings for Rodney, while Gary was still inside the prison awaiting trial.

Yet somehow, she knew now that she would not concede to her feelings for Rodney, and she would continue things with Gary for the moment. Uncoupling a living arrangement can be hard, but she needed to figure out what to do, what would be best for her.

Besides, she never felt that uncoupling from one person should automatically lead to a future with someone else. She knew that much about life, even though she certainly didn't know everything.

She has regrets for sure, but now is not the time to try to sort them out. She is just trying to keep her sanity and keep everything together and it's not easy.

That Friday, she had two gluten-free pizzas and a smoothie, and never made it to the swimming pool.

Chapter 8

Gary did have a secret, however, to show at the right time, which he thought foolishly may be his get out of jail quick card.

He didn't know when, or if, the right time had come to reveal it. And whether it should be disclosed to his lawyer or the police when the time came. He looked around the police station and shuddered. The police station was still cold and damp, and the interview room was almost bare, with scarcely a table and chairs, and a screen to separate the space between the police officer questioning and the interviewee. The interior wall clearly hadn't been painted for decades.

Gary decided he would make a comment to the police and his lawyer.

He didn't know then if he was doing the right thing, but he thought that it couldn't be any worse than keeping things bottled up and being accused of drug dealing when nothing could be further from the truth.

"Okay, Mr. Skater," Gary started, "this is strictly off the record." He barely realized he had spoken when he heard the words coming out of his mouth.

Gary's hand started sweating slightly, and his face flushed. But he had started now, so he would continue.

"Right?" said Skater.

"I want to make a disclosure about something that's going on at work," Gary blurted out to his brief. Although Gary was a lawyer, he was not a criminal lawyer, and he was not completely comfortable with being in a police station

- certainly not on the wrong side of the law anyway.

He was much more used to dealing with family law cases and planning applications and various other matters to do with the legal profession, but not criminal matters.

"Do you think that would be a wise thing to do?" he continued. "And can you ask the constable to turn off the tapes and videos?

He was smart enough to ensure his brief had requested that the tapes and videos be switched off. But not that smart apparently as he was soon to find out.

Gary was yet to realise that actions have consequences, ones that were personal to him anyway. And here, right now, this very fact, might come back to bite him.

Neil Skater was surprised but didn't miss a beat. He was suddenly interested in his client again. Not that he had ever really lost interest, he was a professional. He was only the duty brief, but there was money in this line of work too.

"Maybe this won't be an open and shut case," he thought. "There might be something that can enhance my career here. Or at least I might get paid a few extra days out of it."

Neil Skater was there looking at his watch, gleefully, remembering he was being paid by the hour or the minute by the state.

Although a duty solicitor, it could be a money spinner for him, standing for Gary, he thought.

Gary didn't know, but Mr. Skater had previously had form for prolonging a case, and dragging it out, when legally it was not robust enough to stand up in court. Gary's case might be the same. But he wasn't to know.

"Go on, what's going on at work, you know you don't have to say, but it is better I have all the facts?" says the lawyer.

"There are some mortgages taken out," said Gary, his head in his hands.

"Financial instruments, they were backed on a property, but the deeds were flawed. Two of the properties didn't exist, you see. And for properties that did exist, the planning was flawed. In any event, the process was improper and the loans were secured unlawfully. They shouldn't have been taken out. But

Chapter 8

we thought if they were paid back, that nobody would get hurt. A colleague and I took a kickback, you see, and the money was routed to a cryptocurrency account. I won't mention names, okay?"

"You're going to need to mention names, okay," said Skater.

"But I was a minor player. So, you see it has nothing at all to do with drugs. But I won't go to prison for that, will I? I promise I am not involved in anything like drugs."

The mere mention of drugs abhorred him dreadfully after what happened during university with the cannabis episode that saw him nearly kicked out. How could he have been so stupid?

"It was only a minor fraud. I know about prison for lawyers."

Gary shuddered again at the thought.

"It's terrible inside, for lawyers, Gary, what were you thinking?"

"I'm not involved in smuggling. I'm not. Honestly, I barely take an aspirin." He lied about the aspirin. "I've never sold as much as a sugar cube in my entire life!"

It was Neil Skater's turn to speak, as he has been listening intently to what Gary has been saying.

"Okay, I get it Gary, really, I do. But you're already in prison. You're already locked up. You don't have bail. You're still getting questioned."

Gary wiped his eyes, and grunted, "I know."

Skater continued, "And judges don't go easy on lawyers, they're expected to be above the law and know better what to do in terms of the right thing. It's possible you might have had an excuse if you were doing drugs, but if it's all about the money as your motivation, then I don't know - it's anybody's guess what the judge might say. Any help you can offer would be greatly appreciated; I would imagine."

Skater motioned for Detective Rodney to come through the locked office to listen to the remainder of the interview.

Skater says, "Gary, you can continue to say what you need to say, and what you just told me about the property business, is probably the best thing for you to share right now."

Constable Rodney, now curious, continuing the interview, says, "what you're going to have to do is co-operate with me here and now, Gary, do you understand? Tell me who your colleague is in this property business. With whatever dealing you're doing."

He had been listening from the far side of the two-way screen after all.

"Is it your girlfriend, Irene, is she involved? I know about her, and we know where she works."

Gary answered.

"She works in a in a real estate company. That's all."

The constable continued.

"We know that much - is she senior there? What's her position?

Gary answered. "No, constable, she's not senior. She's just a secretary. She's not involved at all."

Gary paused. A moment later he continued, after catching his breath.

Gary put his face into his palms again and wiped his brow.

"Calm down Gary, you're not helping yourself," Skater warned.

Rodney continued. "You've got to tell me what happened. Tell me right from the beginning. Then we can decide if we can recommend a plea deal."

Moran, the inspector who had been involved in the arrest, walked in by this stage. "Or if the judge might even hear a plea deal, he may not."

"OK constable here's the thing," said Gary. It's nothing to do with drugs, honestly it hasn't. There were never any assaults, not of any kind. I didn't think it was criminality. I thought we were just doing a business deal. I didn't know it was wrong. Then the crypto-currency account was Suzanne's.

"And I found out the amount of money we were getting from the company supplying default instruments. I realised that taking the money through the cryptocurrency account wasn't the right thing to do. That was when I knew that I should have backed out of the deal.

"What happened next," said Moran.

"But it was too late by then. I was tricked by this woman who I was having an affair with, and now it's all over."

"Come now Gary, you're a smart man and well educated, do you really expect me to believe that you didn't know what you were up to?" The constable, conscious that the Inspector was in the room, was annoyed now

Chapter 8

at Gary's clear duplicity. You're not doing yourself any favors blaming the woman. You're going to have to tell us her name.

"It's Irene's boss, Suzanne, you see. She is a partner in the real estate company. And I took the money when she offered me a piece of the deal, after we got friendly. We play tennis together, you see. Oh, it's all a mess!"

"Did she hack into your computer and make you take over a cryptocurrency account? What's her position?"

"I didn't know really, I didn't."

Mr Skater spoke just then, suddenly realizing that he was on Gary's side, and these admissions could prove very problematic for Gary in the future. And for him, if he was seen not to represent a client properly, regardless of who is paying the bill.

"I'd advise you Gary to stop speaking, for your own good. You're making admissions that you have no requirements to make. If what you say is true, that there's no drug charges that can stick, you would be best recommended to stay quiet about anything else."

"Oh, we know about the fraud, Mr Russell," said the police inspector, who had joined the interview room, now questioning Gary with his junior colleague, Constable Rodney.

"We just wanted to know how deeply you were involved, and now we do. You will be charged for it, make no doubt about it. We're going to keep you in custody, now, and you must stay in the cells. Do you understand?"

"Yes, I understand. Do I get a phone call?"

Chapter 9

Julia, Gary's ex, texted Irene just after she hopped out of the shower. Irene shook her head as she towel-dried her hair and frowned.

I heard about Gary. We need to talk. More maintenance needed for Rosie. Muchas Gratias - Julia.

Damn it anyway.

Irene didn't want Julia to know their private business, at least not if she could help it. Julia had been asking Gary for payments to be increased towards the maintenance of her daughter Rosie for a while now.

While Irene wants to give all this a wide berth and just forget about Gary, she feels a little responsible in an emotional sort of way, even though she was not responsible for their break-up several years ago. She knew he had a daughter and an ex-partner before they got together.

But that had caused no problem for her because she had no intention of having a child anyway, and she thought that fact may otherwise have broken them up.

Hi Julia. Don't have access to Gary's finances. I'll have to work something out for you soon. Take care. Irene.

This is all she needs. A spat with her ex's ex with a child in the middle of the mix – and now Julia needing money for Rosie because she can't make

Chapter 9

ends meet. She agreed that it was difficult for Julia to raise a daughter on her own, especially in London, but she really didn't need to hear details. But Rosie was getting older now and she didn't need as much childcare so surely there can't be that much difficulty.

I do not want to put you on the spot Irene, but I might just bring Rosie to Spain to live as it is cheaper over there and then Gary might not see his daughter again. Certainly, he will not see her if he stops maintenance payments!

The stakes couldn't be higher for Gary and Irene's relationship at this moment in time, not to mention Gary's legal problem. She really didn't need this sort of problem. Irene could possibly get Gary's infidelity with her boss at the real estate firm, Suzanne Baron, but only if he was proved innocent of all wrongdoing. But that was unlikely. Julia causing problems could really escalate things for them and cause them to go into a tailspin in every way imaginable.

She didn't exactly know the circumstances of the affair with Suzanne, because Gary and she hadn't had much of a chance to talk about it, but he was a good-looking man, and possibly weak. After all, he had his head turned. No, she was just making excuses for him - she wouldn't get over it.

She felt guilty for even noticing Rodney at the pool.

It's funny, she thought, how things don't seem to be as simple as they were in her parent's day, when two people just met and fell in love and lived happily ever after. She was young enough to want that, and yet old enough to realise that things aren't always as simple as they could be, or she might want them to be.

But putting all that aside for now, much as she really didn't want to, she felt it her duty to try and help Gary sort things out with Julia in keeping Rosie in the country, even if it meant ruining her own credit to pay their joint bills. Having said that, she didn't have any extra money to spend as her job wasn't as well paid as anyone looking in from the outside might think. She didn't have access to Gary's money. And whatever money he had taken into the cryptocurrency account - well, she didn't know anything about that. It was likely to be the proceeds of crime, if it existed at all, and would be confiscated if proven to be a result of a criminal endeavor.

Sure, they had a joint account for bills, and suchlike but not all his salary went into it and not all hers did either. It's not so much that there was financial inequality of any kind, it's just that as an independent woman, she paid her own way, and she just didn't earn as much as he did.

And of course, he was paying maintenance to Rosie and Julia, so that's where his money went.

She didn't know how long it would take to sort out a court case, if it came to that, and meanwhile he was still in custody.

It was the end of the month, and now she had to pay the mortgage for the two of them on her secretary's salary until all this sorry business was sorted out. Really, it was most unfortunate.

She could kill Gary, really, she could, or at least do him some harm.

Or maybe she couldn't.

But she could think about it anyway, or maybe burning his next pizza if she ever got to have pizza night with him again. She ruminated over the good times as well as the bad.

Funny how one thing and another can have such drastic consequences, and how she really didn't know how serious this was for him in the police station.

Really, how seriously they took a drug possession charge.

She still didn't know what the extent of the fraud was because he hadn't told her before he was arrested, and the phone calls were limited since then. But with Suzanne involved it could be serious.

Irene decided to ring Julia.

Maybe she can find out more on the phone.

The phone rang twice, and Julia answered.

"Hello, Irene?"

Julia must have had Irene's number stored in her phone to have recognised it when it rang, it seemed like she was expecting the call.

"Yeah, it's me Irene. How are you keeping Julia?" Irene started.

"I'm okay. And you?"

"Well things aren't so good with Gary as you know, but I can't say too much about that. I don't know the details."

"I'm sorry for your problems," ventured Julia. "Things are not so good with

Chapter 9

Rosie or my job as it's low paid."

"Are things really so bad that you'd consider going back to Spain with Rosie?" replied Irene. "Gary hasn't been on trial yet, are you sure it's not a bit premature?"

Julia paused and said finally, "I need some money as my job is not well paid, because my English and technology skills are not so good, I'm sorry to say. So yes, I must."

"Oh, that's too bad. I'll see if I can sort something out. Please don't do anything hasty. You promise me, Julia?"

"Sure Irene, if you can get me money for rent and bills, I stay, but otherwise I must go back to my country. It's so expensive here."

Irene and Julia hung up from their phone call and Irene then sent a message to Gary's brief to fill him in on proceedings. Gary rang her back when he's allowed to make a phone call.

"Irene, what's up?" he said. "I heard you wanted to talk. I'm miserable in here."

"Sorry to drop this on you, Gary. Julia is looking for more money, for Rosie. She is threatening to take her to Spain if she doesn't get it, and you might not see her again."

It looks like Gary and Irene are getting on better, but the issues between them are far from resolved.

Gary still hadn't been bailed yet, and he didn't know if that was a realistic prospect, because his brief was still working out the details. A hundred thousand pounds is hard to come by, even for Gary.

So, Irene is still on her own sorting out this sorry mess.

What about your parents? Can they help? Irene suggested when she found out that Gary's bank accounts had been frozen temporarily, along with his only asset worth anything - his Harley-Davidson.

Or what about your law firm, Gary? Could they give you a loan perhaps?

"Doesn't look likely, Irene, as they appear to have frozen me out because I'm in jail, and now I have no source of income. Being in the law profession means I'm supposed to be above reproach, and even though they don't know what's going on and I haven't been convicted of anything, there's an assumption that I'm guilty."

"I'll try your mother for a loan on your behalf, but I can't promise anything."

"Thanks Irene, I appreciate all your help. I don't know what I'd do without you."

"You might have to make do without me soon enough because this doesn't mean we're okay." Irene was still angry. "I still don't know the full story about what went on with you and Suzanne and this fraud of yours."

"Really Irene, it hasn't been what you think. But I know it's been rough on you. I'm sorry for everything."

"Yeah, it has, Gary," said Irene. "I realise I probably didn't know you at all." She said it with a note of finality in her voice that, although it was quivering a little, told her she was finally moving on.

Chapter 10

Gary's mother may have been the more approachable of his two parents and Irene had only met her on one or two occasions, so she was more than a little nervous.

The first time she met Gary's parents was in their large sprawling house in Essex and she had to be on her best behaviour for high tea. Although it was only two years ago now, it sure seemed like an age. Even though she had changed, and grown closer to Gary, she really didn't know that much about his parents. He didn't talk about them much, having had problems with his dad over the years.

But for the sake of Gary's daughter Rosie, Irene decided to make the request to Gary's mother over a coffee date near their home. She chose somewhere neutral, so she wouldn't feel so isolated if things didn't go so well. She hadn't met the lady in a long time and their upbringings had been completely different. Gary's mum was a lady who lunches who had married well, rather than someone who has worked their way up through the ranks, like Irene's mum had. Different family styles, that was certain.

Not to mention the fact that there were 30 years in age between Irene and Gary's mum. Yes, it would be an awkward meeting, she knew that. But Irene would do it for the sake of Rosie. She really did care for that little girl who she'd practically been a stepmother to for the last couple of years.

Irene decided to wear a floral autumnal coloured dress to suit the season with a pair of dark ankle boots, as Gary's mother is quite conservative, and she insists on being called Ms Russell. Irene was sure she would be well turned out for their meeting.

She doesn't want to cause any unnecessary offence by choosing the wrong outfit. Irene remembers that Gary's mother wears skirt separates, and a highly made-up face. She also wore perfume and muted nail polish over her natural nails. Irene and Gary might be breaking up, but she will not let herself down now, not in front of Ms Russell.

She wondered what she'd tell Ms. Russell about the impending breakup or if the conversation about that would.happen at all. So many questions were up in the air right now, so it was difficult to understand exactly what she should say. But in the end, it was Gary's mum who spoke first.

They were in a little coffee shop and Gary's mum had ordered two coffees for them to drink, as they had arrived at the same time.

Gary's mum was very chatty when they met and put her at ease immediately.

The conversation began oddly at first with the older lady talking about a party she had been to, where she was asked who would kill the guest of honour at their 100th birthday party?

"Just for a joke," she said, "the conversation had started, but it quickly turned into a full-on discussion. I mean really! This was a topic of discussion among her book club book club ladies who were having a chat about it one day. Apparently, it was the plot of some book they had read. Not too well received. They scoffed at it, but she thought it was a decent crime caper, nonetheless. It had a strange plot and a plot twist at the end."

Irene wondered why she was telling her this story, but her wait to begin the discussion of why they were meeting would soon be over.

Irene relaxed and drank her coffee as her companion continued talking. Clearly, she didn't know about Gary.

"Now what did you want to see me about dear?" Gary's mum said finally, I know there's something."

Irene didn't know how to broach the subject.

Chapter 10

But finally, she blurted out, "I'm sorry, Ms Russell, I need money for Gary's legal fees and to pay the things he needs to pay. Money is tight and we have been stretched to the limit on their mortgage. And Rosie needs money too."

But nobody really wants to hear about money troubles. Irene really didn't want to be talking about them either. And yet here she was, talking to Ms. Russell like she was an old friend.

"I'm so sorry Irene, she says, it must have been a wasted trip for you. I don't have access to any money unfortunately, and Gary's father, well, he won't hear of bailing him out right now. He's so upset with the situation, he really is."

"Oh, that's a shame, really it is," says Irene. "I hoped Gary's father would look more favourably on him now. But I suppose it's hard to keep faith if you're being let down."

"It's not Rosie, you understand. We're very fond of that girl - our first grandchild - but Gary's father, like I said, won't hear of helping him out financially."

Irene was disappointed but she didn't skip a beat. She suddenly saw a little insight into the inside the marriage of Gary's parents. His mother and father did not appear to function as one.

Or maybe it seemed that way to her because she'd asked a favour and his mum was unable to help her out, not even for her son.

Ms. Russell explained that her husband held the cheque book and refused to let her help his son, no matter how much she wanted to - there was one favourite brother and that was not Gary. So, it looks like this avenue of wealth does not spring eternal, and it appears to be a dead end!

Gary's father William made sure that his mother could not give a financial dig-out to her son, even if she wanted to. Her husband controlled the bank accounts and all the financial purse strings in this household.

It was an odd arrangement really, Irene thought, later, as she went home empty-handed.

After making such an effort to wear the right outfit, with makeup and nails and make a good impression, it didn't exactly matter what she wore in the end. Gary's dad has put his foot down before she'd arrived and had hidden her cheque book.

Gary's mum had worn a suit separates as Irene assumed she would, but although she looked every bit the businessperson, in this event, it didn't make any difference. She didn't have access to the money her family had, and even if she did, she may not have wanted to give it to him.

So, it looked like Gary was on his own in the family. And appearing not to have any support except for Irene.

What would happen with Rosie now? Spain isn't too far away in the world, of course, even the little coastal village an hour south of Barcelona that Julia came from. But that didn't mean it wouldn't be difficult for Gary to see her anymore. He was devoted to her, but then again, he might be facing a lengthy jail sentence.

And as Irene kept reminding herself, (as if her thoughts would somehow be sent to Gary telepathically), actions have consequences and who knows where he would end up.

And what would happen in the court case? The truth had yet to be uncovered, Irene thought. And she really didn't know what to do about it at this juncture in time, she still was confused.

Who could she talk to about this? Who could she confide in? At least she had her swimming, she needed to clear head in the pool and feel like she was in control of something in her life even if it wasn't that much.

She telephoned Grace that evening for a chat and check-in. She has been so busy covering for Suzanne at work lately that they hadn't had much of a chance to have coffee together.

"Hi Grace," said Irene, "how are you doing stranger? It's been such a long time since we've had a chance to catch up, we must go for a walk together soon! Or shopping - it's so long since we had the chance to catch up over some retail therapy."

"Yes of course," said Grace. "Is everything OK with you though? It's been so long since you rang me. I'm just concerned you're out of sorts. You haven't been yourself in the office. Are you distracted, or just busy?"

"What, me? No. I'm fine," said Irene.

"Well, it hasn't been that easy since Suzanne left, I'm covering a lot of the

Chapter 10

things she used to do. And I get none of the credit. Plus, with Gary gone, it's harder at home to manage. I know it's only been a couple of weeks. But still. It's not easy."

"Yes, that must be true," said Grace. "Let's do lunch and then we can have a proper chat soon."

Chapter 11

Julia left a cryptic message for Irene on her answer phone overnight, telling her that she will be leaving for Spain early in the morning on the seven o'clock flight to Barcelona on a chartered plane.

Hi Irene, it's Julia. I'm going to Barcelona tomorrow on a chartered plane at 7:00 in the morning with Rosie and I won't be back. If you need to get in touch, it's best if we do it through a lawyer, as you have not seen to be able to get any further maintenance money for me and Rosie, and Gary seems not to be able to answer the phone anymore.

She said she wouldn't be back anytime soon, and everything must now be done through lawyers. She had heard about the situation with Gary. Now she feared that Gary was involved with drugs and that he would be a poor influence on his daughter Rosie.

Irene got the message late at night after her gym workout and it was too late to ring back. She did a little research of her own on her phone and found out the flight details and decided to go to the airport to meet Julia. She wanted the chance to give her own side of the own story and perhaps to persuade her not to go away so suddenly. And so permanently.

They meet at the check-in desk of the chartered flight. Irene didn't want to cause a scene, not in front of Rosie anyway, and she knew enough about airports that she would be fearful of doing anything untoward in an airport.

Chapter 11

"Julia is there any chance you might change your mind about this matter?" said Irene when she caught up with Julia. "I mean going away. With Rosie. I'm not sure what you've heard about Gary, but he's not been involved in drug dealing, I can tell you that. I honestly don't know what he's been involved in, but he hates drugs, he always has, and you know that."

"I always thought that", says Julia, "but now I'm not so sure. I really need to get away. You shouldn't have come to the airport."

"Are you sure I can't persuade you to stay?"

"No Irene, you can't. My luggage is packed, I've got my tickets, I've given up my apartment, which I can't afford anyway. I'm expected in Spain. That's it."

With that, she walked away past security with Rosie.

Julia planned to take her daughter to Spain, to her parents' family, and said Gary will never see her again, at least not for a while. She might consider access if payments were restored, and if he agreed to meet her in Spain.

"I really know this will be difficult, but there is nothing further to say."

Nothing Irene could do would change Julia's mind. Gary would be heartbroken, Irene knew, but at the end of the day, all of this was his own doing, so she cannot be responsible. She didn't know about Julia's breakup with Gary, whether that was his fault. But this problem, this trouble he was in with the law, appeared to be his fault. Even if he wasn't fully culpable, he must take responsibility. But it was just unfortunate that his daughter was caught in the crossfire.

"Rosie, will you be a good girl for mama in Spain?" Irene said to the little girl before she went past security with Julia.

Rosie, nearly a teenager, was a lovely young girl who Irene had come to know well over the past two years.

"I'll be good," Rosie said, "and I'll see you Irene soon, I really hope you can visit. Even if dad can't. I really missed dad," she continued tearfully.

It nearly breaks Irene's heart to watch her young charge go.

Rosie was on her way to the little town outside Barcelona where her family's Spanish homestead is, far away from London. And far away from Irene and Gary.

Not long after, the tall, handsome police officer Rodney soon appeared at the airport terminal from which Irene was too distraught to leave. Julia and Rosie's flight to Spain had departed and they were now on their way to Spain.

Rodney and Irene began to chat although at the smoothie bar, he had just asked her for an interview to clear up a few questions down at the station.

Irene remarks to herself that at her partner's arrest is the most unromantic place to meet a new love interest in her life. She didn't say that aloud, did she?

But it appears that this may have been the case because she can't stop thinking about Rodney and she wondered if it might be that he feels the same about her. It must be inappropriate, though, to get involved with a woman he has met at an arrest? And for Irene, it sure feels like she is betraying Gary, who has in turn betrayed her in so many ways.

Even so, she cannot possibly feel guilty. But for all that, she realises how easy it is to get involved with someone else, when you think that all is going well at home.

How quickly things can turn around for a couple, involved with such a routine life. How quickly things like security can be turned around and flipped.

Irene was a little obsessed with trying to figure out her feelings and how they fit in with the reality of the situation with Gary.

"There's been some developments," said Rodney.

"What do you mean?" Irene replied.

"I mean we figured out that Gary isn't dealing drugs after all, and we might be able to bail him out at some stage soon."

"Oh, that's great news, officer."

"However, there is a bigger investigation going on in which he's also involved, and we might be needing to question you about that matter. Can you make yourself available at short notice for questioning?" Rodney asked. "And please don't leave the airport by plane, or any port authority for that matter. We need you to stay in the jurisdiction."

"What's this about? I'm not involved in anything, and I don't know anything about Gary's involvement in anything dodgy either! Do I really need to watch my movements and are you going to be following me? Was it really a

Chapter 11

coincidence that you were at the gym when I was there the other week?"

"Relax, Irene. Call me Rodney," he smiled. "Oh, I didn't even notice. Were you there? Oh yes, I bumped into you at the shop afterwards. I'd forgotten about that. But don't worry, it's quite routine."

"Oh, thank goodness for that."

"No, we won't be following you, but we will be asking you in for a few questions or we will arrange for an interview with you at a mutual time of convenience for both of us. It's nothing to worry about really, it's not."

Rodney sidles off to another part of the airport, leaving Irene to figure out exactly what happened.

She'd never even spoken to a police officer before she met Rodney and his boss the other day during Gary's arrest, and she made sure she didn't talk too much after the pool meeting.

Or had it been a few weeks? She really didn't know.

Irene was losing track of time, and she wasn't up to her peak performance, either professionally or personally.

She had been showing up for work at the real estate agency, however, so at least she was taking care of business, even though her head was not exactly in the game.

Suzanne, appeared to be a missing person.

She seemed to have disappeared soon after Gary's arrest and the scene at the apartment.

But at least now Irene knew for sure that it's not Gary's fault because he wasn't dealing, and he wasn't using drugs. She still thinks this. She had been conflicted before. Well of course she was still conflicted, what with Rosie and Julia, and Spain, and Gary and, oh, it's all a mess.

Irene has tried her best to help Gary with the money for his daughter, which she did not get from his mother. Her mortgage is due, but at least she's getting a regular salary from the real estate agency. For now.

But now she felt like she had failed because she did not keep Julia from taking Rosie out of the country.

What would she tell Gary when he rang, he's going to be distraught about his daughter? But he was just being self-centered and only looking after himself, Irene didn't know.

The monthly event at the tennis club had been a roaring success that Saturday. Even without Gary. Irene had brought Grace, her friend from the office, just to see how things panned out and she wasn't disappointed because there were a lot of new tennis events, and new people in attendance whom she hadn't expected to meet.

Irene and Gary had planned to attend together. It was to be the biggest day of the Autumn schedule when all the touring players come and, the major tournament takes place in the club, but with things the way they were now Irene wasn't so sure what to think.

Irene thought she saw Suzanne later, dancing. But she couldn't be that stupid, really, could she? Appearing here of all places.

She might have been trying a double bluff and attempting to make sure everyone knew she hadn't done anything untoward.

In fairness, though, it was Gary amid the investigation, and she wasn't so sure that Suzanne was even under investigation.

Not under investigation yet, she thought.

She then thought of what Rodney had said earlier at the airport, about having to answer questions at the police station and she shuddered.

Not ever having been questioned before by a police officer, she really didn't know what to expect.

Would it be all business with Rodney, or would she get to chat over, for example, a cup of coffee? Or would she be in handcuffs, or in a locked room? She really didn't have any idea what they thought she was involved in.

"You seem to have a lot on your mind Irene," said Grace. "Is there anything I can help you with?"

"Not so much. I really don't want to talk about it but, truth be told Grace I'm really at a loose end and I don't know what to do."

She began to fill her in on the happenings of the month, since they had taken an early lunch break to go shopping before the previous Tennis Club event. They hadn't had a chance to catch up for that walk, or the coffee.

Grace was flabbergasted.

"Oh my gosh, Irene, what did you do?" said Grace when she heard the story

Chapter 11

about the arrest. "And, Suzanne, I was wondering why she was missing from the office. I can't imagine how she could bear to show her face at work after that. But she is brazen. I always suspected that".

"Well," continued Irene, glad to have an audience for her misery. "I was very upset at first, but then I just continued with my life. I've been managing. I went swimming. I contacted Gary's mum to see if she could help with his bail money and with money for his daughter, but she couldn't. Beyond that, I haven't been able to do that much besides, you know, being me. You know what I mean Grace, that's what I do. I manage. I manage things. But guess what, I must go to Scotland Yard or some local police station, I'm not sure where, to give a statement about what's been going on. I don't know what to do about it. Do you have any suggestions for how to act?"

"When do you have to be interviewed," retorted Grace, exceedingly curious. "I bet you're not happy about that! What are you going to wear?"

"To the police station? I don't know. I haven't thought about it. That's the least of my worries, Grace. Bigger picture stuff is in my head. Rosie is going to Spain to some tiny little town where she doesn't know anybody. And where she doesn't know anyone, and Gary's facing a jail sentence. I really don't see why what I'm going to wear makes any difference."

But in the back of her mind Irene did worry about what she wore. She worried about what she looked like, and she had anxiety which caused her a great deal of angst.

Gary knew it, and supported her, without judging and that was probably why she continued to stick by him. He had stood by her through the early days when she was going through feelings of anxiety before she felt as comfortable as she seemed to at this moment in time.

But with Gary in prison, all she wanted to do now was swim and eat and drink and that was never going to be a good combination. Irene needs to feel control over her life, but she's not in control and can never be fully in control.

Irene chatted to a few of Gary's work colleagues at the Tennis Club who asked after him, but they were just curious to know what happened with him. The news had made the papers and although Gary's name hadn't been mentioned, there were rumours because his profession had been disclosed, as had the charges that this unnamed professional was facing.

Irene was sure they were just looking for information or being nasty. So, she made sure she didn't give them any information. One of the men asked for her for a dance afterward, but she was sure he was joking.

Who dances these days, she thought? Especially with a colleague's partner. Who knows what he was thinking, in fairness?

Irene then thought of Gary and Suzanne, and was again down hearted, thinking of the situation as it had happened. Then her mind wandered again to the swimming pool, and Rodney.

Chapter 12

On the Tuesday of the following week after the meeting in the airport, Irene went to the police station as planned, in the early evening. Constable Rodney had made the appointment for her to go in, and she attended after work.

She was to be questioned, but she didn't yet know what she was to be questioned about.

She was assured that she didn't need a lawyer as she wasn't under investigation, but she was just to help the officers out with their inquiries and to see if there was any information she could share on any of the issues that had come to light.

Yeah right, Irene thought.

But she knew she needed to answer the questions, otherwise she would be implicated herself. She had to clear her name which, in fairness, she understood to be clear already. According to Constable Rodney, she was here purely to answer questions about Gary. And Suzanne of course, if they wanted to know. She wanted them to know, of course, about Suzanne, and so would they if they wanted the full picture. She certainly intended to give them the full picture anyway.

Irene arrived at the police station and asked the desk Sergeant if she could speak to constable Rodney Mooney. He had given her his full name earlier when he had asked her for the interview and set it up by telephone.

He now had her telephone number and full name, and he knew where she lived. Irene Harley from Richmond upon Thames in southwest London.

She felt a tiny bit exposed.

But then again, she knew his full name and the station where he worked, and she could complain if he didn't treat her correctly during the interview.

At least that was what she was led to believe, when her rights were being conveyed to her.

"Take a seat Irene," said constable Rodney, as he brought her into a small conference room. "Would you like a coffee, a cup of tea or a glass of water? This is an informal interview by the way; we're just asking you a few questions to see if you can help us."

Rodney brought Irene into a room with a pinewood conference table where eight people could meet, and there were comfortable chairs around it for seating. Also, in the conference room, there appeared to be closed circuit television cameras, a laptop computer, and a projection screen. The inspector who had questioned Gary was already seated when Irene and Rodney entered the room.

"I thought this was an informal meeting," said Irene a little worried. I'm not so sure talking to you is such a clever idea.

Rodney spoke reassuringly.

"Well, honestly Irene, it would be better to get the full story sooner rather than later, and your side of things would be helpful to have. You can give an insight into the main parties involved in this; we'd really like to have your opinion on the record. And the facts as you know them of course."

"Well, okay, then," said Irene. I'll have a coffee, and this is an informal chat, I hope. Because I was advised that I could have a lawyer present, but I don't see the need for that because I genuinely didn't know what was happening until the day when you came through the door of the apartment to arrest Gary, and that's the truth."

The inspector speaks next.

"That's fine Irene. Yes, it is an informal chat. We've got to find the

Chapter 12

underlying cause of this, because it is a news story, and there is a crime at the centre. You must have seen it in the papers, even though Gary's name wasn't mentioned. It's a live case and a live investigation. But make no mistakes Miss, it is serious. And any help you can give also in relation to the matter at hand will be helpful."

Rodney went over to a sideboard in the conference room and brought back a coffee to Irene in a china cup. He handed another one to the inspector. There was milk in a stainless-steel jug, beside a small plate of biscuits. If this was an attempt to side-track Irene into making unplanned disclosures and unsettle her, well, it hadn't worked - yet.

But she hadn't spoken, yet, either.

Irene spoke.

"So, what do you want to know?" she started, a little nervous.

"How long have you known Gary? Are you sharing that apartment for long?"

"Well," said Irene, after a brief pause to gather her thoughts. She wanted to help them and make sure she didn't say anything she would regret.

"I'd say Gary is my partner for the last two years, romantic partner that is. We met online on a dating app, and moved in together shortly thereafter, and I know he works in an office in town because we travel in on the underground train together on our commute. We work on opposite sides of the same street in central London. We have a mortgage on the apartment. He has a daughter from an earlier relationship. What else do you want to know?"

"Who pays maintenance?" asked the inspector.

"Gary pays. He has financial commitments for his daughter, but he tries to be a good father."

The inspector speaks again.

"Yes, we're sure he's a good father, well we're not sure. We're just trying to find out more. Whether or not he's a good father isn't really the point, is it?"

Irene, getting a little frustrated continued, "Well what is the point? I'm telling you what I know and I'm answering your questions, and I don't know what else to say."

"Do you know anything about real estate? Mortgages on properties?

Planning applications?"

"I know a little about real estate," replied Irene. "But honestly, I'm just a secretary at the real estate firm where I work, and the only thing I know about mortgages is how to pay the one on my own apartment. I don't know anything about planning applications. It's a different department in the real estate company where I work, I don't get to see anything.

"I've been occasionally asked to go out to a copy shop, and get maps duplicated in large print facsimile, but I have no reason to believe that anything like that was out of the ordinary for the line of business I worked in. Honestly, officers I had no idea. If that has anything to do with what you're investigating, I honestly didn't know anything about it."

"Did you ever talk about your work to Gary for instance?" Rodney asked quietly.

"Sure, we chatted. General chit chat about work. But it's never been the case that I thought that he was listening to me in any way that was out of the ordinary and scheming behind my back to get some financial gain out of my work. I'm honestly not sure if my clients and his clients were the same people, or the same buildings. It's possible they were. But if there were similarities in clients and commercial buildings, I certainly didn't know about it."

"Did Gary talk about his work, over dinner, or on dates for example?" asked Rodney, probing.

"No. Gary was incredibly careful not to talk about his work anyway. Not at home. Not on dates, and certainly not out in public. I knew he wasn't involved in criminal law, but I thought it was family law, or personal injury. I wasn't that aware if he was involved, and if what he was doing had anything to do with commercial real estate, to be honest with you. Really, I wasn't."

"Okay, Irene, you're doing really well," Rodney reassured her.

"Can I ask you if Gary did drugs, or if he had ever done drugs? Have you ever taken drugs." It was the inspector who spoke that time.

She was shocked at the question because she never had.

She had been prescribed some anxiety medication when she was a teenager, and she took paracetamol the whole time for a headache but that was about it.

Chapter 12

The inspector persisted with the questioning, because he was sure she knew something more, and he was sure she was involved somehow.

By now, Irene was getting adrenaline flushes in her cheeks and feeling palpitations.

Rodney tried to calm her and assured her everything would be okay. And that she didn't need to worry if she just continued to answer the questions.

"Am I free to go officers," she said finally.

"You're not accused of anything, Miss Harley," replied the inspector. "You are just helping us with our inquiries."

"So," continued Irene, "if I want to go then I can?".

"Yes."

"Well, I think I will go then, if there's nothing further."

And she left.

She couldn't help thinking about Suzanne though and she knew there's something wasn't right. Why else would they be talking about drugs the whole time?

She began to suspect gambling because there was no money left in his accounts and he couldn't afford his bills. She didn't know much about the cryptocurrency until she went investigating. And once she went investigating, she found all sorts of evidence on their personal computer, in a computer file protected only by Gary's birth-date.

But Irene hadn't been asked about that. So, she didn't volunteer the information either.

Chapter 13

Irene continued to go to the office in central London after the police interview with Rodney and the inspector. She continued to pay the bills, and life as it had been, appeared to continue to go on as normal. She went to the gym to use the swimming pool, and occasionally she saw Rodney there teaching lessons to the young teenagers. She knew by now that he went on Tuesdays and Fridays, and sometimes she changed her schedule to suit his so that she might bump into him. Things weren't going so great with Gary at home.

To distract from everything that was going on in the office and at home, Irene madly decided to adopt a dog from the local shelter, but she didn't realize at the time that the management company wasn't exactly enamored with the idea of dogs on the premises and it was against the rules.

It did give her a chance to get active during the times that she was not already out, so now she walked the dog twice a day as well as everything else she was managing. Truth be told, she might have been too busy, having too many things on her plate. Regardless, she was managing – that was what she did.

She really likes the dog. And in fairness, the dog chose her when she went to the shelter to check to see if she could get one. In the end she got a small cocker-spaniel with a snub nose about two-years-old and full of life. She was asked what she should name him, if she wanted to change his name for any

Chapter 13

reason. She said no, and she called him Sandy because he had a name tag that said Sandy, and she didn't want to change the dog's name.

She was advised to change it because he might remember his old life before the shelter. But she thought he looked well enough adjusted that she wouldn't change his name, so she didn't.

A few weeks later, she noticed an advertisement in a local shop window to say the dog was missing. And that the dog's name was Sandy. Or her name was Sandy. Sandy could be a male dog or a female. Irene wasn't entirely sure about these things. She recognized the dog in the photo and the name on the name tag. So, she was a little bit devastated. Just a bit.

And then she thought she should really ring the number and find out if the dog and the owner on the flier belonged together.

She spoke to Rodney about it first.

And he told her the same thing, that she should really contact the owner.

She had to give the dog up, and it was nearly as upsetting as saying goodbye to Rosie at the airport.

Meanwhile, back in the office, life went on for Irene, and she continued to restrict her food and prepared gluten free pizza for dinners the occasional night with her swimming regimen, to control the only things she can control. Her anxiety is leading to her not eating more of the time, and she was getting a little weaker. But nobody noticed. Least of all Irene. Rodney did, but he didn't say anything.

He doesn't feel it's his place to intervene in Irene's life yet. But he knew he wanted to keep an eye on it, and he wanted to keep an eye on Irene. Gary was just self-absorbed and didn't think about anything except what was going on with him and his own self-inflicted problems.

Irene sometimes fantasized about going on a date with Rodney and remembered his casual and easy manner when they had met at the smoothie bar that time weeks ago. That day she barely spoke to him. The day Gary was arrested.

By then, Gary had been bailed and was awaiting his court appearance.

But all had changed for Gary.

Because of his dalliance with Suzanne, and the fraud that he was now being charged with, he had lost a lot. He had to surrender his passport, so he couldn't go to Spain to visit his daughter, and now he missed her dreadfully.

Not only that, but he was no longer allowed to practise law at work and had lost his ability to earn an income from going into the office every day.

He was suspended from client work and told not to go into the office pending the outcome of the legal investigation.

He was also in danger of being struck off the law register, or at least suspended for quite a considerable period. Quite besides, of course, in the worst-case scenario, the possibility of a lengthy jail sentence.

So, his problems with Irene were causing difficulties but they weren't the biggest of either of them. Irene didn't seem to care, and Gary questioned this. He was devastated that she wasn't his biggest supporter anymore, and he appeared not to have any insight into why that might be.

"Don't you care about working on our relationship," he would say to Irene over breakfast, for instance.

"Oh, I'm busy, too busy to have this conversation right now. Honestly, the relationship is the least of my worries. I'm sorry, but we'll have to talk later."

She knew she was being unfair, not to let him know exactly where he stood, but being unconfrontational was her style.

She had let things seem unimportant after she had initially blown up in anger when she found out about Suzanne.

After that, she seemed to let things go, and not to care so much. Or perhaps it was a cover, and she really did care, but she was just parking her feelings, until she could deal with them at a later stage.

Irene was more worried about work now anyway.

Meanwhile, she made presentations to the clients and did all the work that Suzanne had been doing prior to her absence following Gary's arrest. The partners in the company appeared appreciative. It seemed like all the bosses shared this feeling, but they didn't tell Irene that they appreciated her in so many words. It appeared they expected her to be a mind reader.

She never got any bonus for staying late or missing any of her scheduled appointments, which she occasionally had to do because of her commitments in the office. She had begun seeing a counsellor a while ago and found it

Chapter 13

beneficial, but now she was missing the meetings because of unexpected deadlines.

She was a little annoyed sometimes because she wasn't getting a bonus or recognised as Suzanne had been as a partner. She was no longer just a secretary, she knew that. But was anyone else ever going to realise that? She was really coming into her own in the real estate business. At this stage, she wasn't sure what the future would hold at this stage when this was all over.

As for the planning permits for the building that Irene had been researching prior to all these happenings. She now realised that all this fraud was in the planning of the same buildings. The fraud with the permits for the buildings and the mortgage kickbacks in cryptocurrency were all in the planning with Gary and Suzanne. It was part of their affair. She wondered which came first, the affair or the scam. Perhaps, it didn't matter.

She could see for herself that Gary wasn't on drugs, and he wasn't a drug dealer. She knew that. She knew as much during the interview with Rodney on the inspector. Even they basically admitted that.

But now she realized exactly which building it had been because Suzanne hadn't been able to cover her tracks until then, and it appeared she hadn't destroyed evidence from the computer yet or taken away her desktop and phones.

It's possible, the other partners still thought Suzanne was coming back, and they really didn't know where she was, but if they did know, they never said. Irene suspected it was up to her to say what she knew to the partners, but she knew in the end that it wasn't her place.

But she couldn't help remembering Rodney, and the sobering interview that she did at the police station about any involvement of hers, and anything she might know about Gary. It had really changed her. She didn't know anything about cryptocurrency or cybercrime or planning permits.

All she knew about was how to get the job done that she was asked to do, to manage, and how to tell the truth. She was essentially an ethical person, and all this criminal drama and upset in her life was very disturbing and really made her uneasy.

Meanwhile, she continued in the gym. She continued making pizza on

Friday nights. She continued her swimming. And she continued her five-a-side soccer with a small team from work. For now, anyway.

But her anxiety was getting the better of her occasionally, and she was slowly heading for, she didn't know what, maybe, a breakdown?

She had an experience in college a few years back where she didn't cope so well with what was going on in her life, and she wound up in a health facility for teenagers who had problems. And when she told Gary about this, he had been more supportive than her earlier boyfriend who broke up with her. She couldn't help wondering now if her loyalty to Gary was misplaced.

Maybe she needed a little space and time away from the situation, to get a breakaway for a weekend. A little headspace if you will.

Chapter 14

"So, what are you going to wear to court Gary?" said Irene, during a moment when herself and Gary were being civil and talking. "What did your brief advise?"

"It's hard to say. I don't know what's best really. If I go in a suit, it'll look like I'm a real white-collar criminal, if I go casual it'll look like I might be a drug user after all. I really don't have all the answers. Maybe I'll go smart casual like what I wear to the office on Fridays - used to wear to the office on Friday, that is."

"Well, the court date is on Friday so maybe that would work," said Irene.

"Why don't we have a last meal together, just for old times' sake?" asked Gary hopefully. Just in case, well you know, just in case I end up behind bars again. I don't want to say it, but it could happen. So, what's it to be? Chinese takeaway and a bottle of wine? On Thursday night instead maybe?

"Okay, sounds good. We'll have a Chinese. I'm sure there's something I can find on the menu that I can eat. A final meal for the convicted criminal," joked Irene.

"Oh, don't say that!" said Gary worriedly.

"Remember we used to enjoy these date nights immensely. I'm sure it'll be back to normal soon," he continued, although he wasn't so sure he believed it himself.

Irene was looking forward to the court date, although she didn't admit it. And she didn't say that to Gary. She had a bit of space on her own while he was in prison, and maybe a bit of space to evaluate where she was going. Yes, she was anxious about Rosie and her future.

And, about herself, and where she was going in the world. But she had also been thinking about her parents lately. Maybe she should give them a visit.

The court date was looming. If there was press in the courtroom, as there often were in planning cases (and drug cases, for that matter), perhaps she was just as well to stay away. She had her reputation to think of, and she was known in the financial district. She really didn't want to be seen in court.

On the other hand, she knew from Rodney there were no drugs charges now, and that they wouldn't stand up in court even if they were mentioned. However, she wasn't honestly sure what the judge would say, as this matter hadn't been brought up before now the court, the police bail had been given to Gary without objection in the end. And this was the actual trial. A very different matter.

There was only so much support she was prepared to give Gary. Irene was no shrinking violet, she knew her own mind, and she had a good idea of court procedures from her voluminous interest in police procedurals. She imagined that was reality anyway or was it just TV.

Maybe it would be good for Gary to see that there wasn't endless support for him from Irene. She had to keep the house going at home. Basically, she was doing what was important, she was earning a living and supporting him from afar. She kept in touch with Julia about Rosie, but even those texts and phone calls were getting further and further apart, and Irene seemed less and less interested in making things up with Gary.

Not only that, but Gary didn't know what all of this was doing to her anxiety levels. He could only think about himself right now. And now his court case was the most important thing, so maybe it made sense that she wasn't there.

She needed to make a stand about something and maybe this was it.

Chapter 15

Julia's obsession with money and extracting it from Gary is preying on Irene's sensibilities even though she and Gary are no longer an item.

They're still sharing living space and have yet to formally uncouple. Gary's very sad about this as it seems that he's made a big mistake and he's being punished with a very big price for it.

But he still hasn't faced up to his gambling problem and the loans that have been secured on the non-existent buildings. Well, who knows what's going to happen with them. Buildings will always exist. But the question of who owns what and who's secured what loans on which, well, that's a matter for legal challenge and Gary has been legally challenged, that's for sure.

But Julia, she's a little obsessed with being cruel now to Gary in his hour of darkness. Irene tries to bring her back to her senses and Rosie is again stuck in the middle.

Julia is now communicating with Irene from Spain via email from a Spanish solicitor, but it looks like she may be back in London quite soon.

Although she has only given unclear reasons for this so far, she says that Rosie is having blood tests and it may lead to some sort of childhood diagnosis which, depending on the outcome, could be serious and could lead to her having greater financial needs that are genuine this time.

Irene rolls her eyes when she hears this, although genuinely, she would love to see Rosie, the little girl she has cared for and who now may be unwell.

She wonders what the problem could be and vows to help her if she can.

Earlier Irene had been doing well. She was doing well at work and managing to do everything that was needed to keep her on balance and in check for her greatest level of well-being. This included swimming and regular eating. Plus, there was an online support group that she used to attend, which she occasionally checked in on even now.

But Suzanne had been missing in action from the firm lately, and Irene doesn't know what is proper to say or what not to say.

Irene heard a rumour by the water cooler that she's been seen at a health spa in the Midlands. Meanwhile, Irene has been working as hard as she could, trying to keep up with everything and managing to fail spectacularly at most of the personal obligations that she had made to herself, that usually kept her out of harm's way.

Her swimming has now gone by the wayside. She hasn't been on five-a-side soccer in weeks, and she still hasn't managed to track down Julia, who hasn't answered her phone since she took Rosie out of the country.

What could go wrong that hasn't happened already? She thought she was doing fine at work, especially after she covered Suzanne's work for a few weeks as well as her own. But now she wasn't so sure.

One Monday morning right after the weekly planning meeting, one of the partners called Irene into his office. The managing partner Mr Austin is an older gentleman in his sixties and Suzanne, Irene's boss has normally reported directly to him. She always thought he was kindly in nature, but she also knew that he had a streak that meant he wanted to get things done just so - and he knew how he liked things to be.

"So, Irene, do you have anything to tell me about why you've been distracted lately?" he inquired.

"Not so much Mr Austin," she said in reply, a little puzzled as to why she had been called in to speak to the top boss. "I'm not sure what you mean about distraction. I thought I've been doing all the work needed and covering for Suzanne as well. Why is Suzanne away, and how long will she be gone for?" she said.

She felt bold asking this question. It seemed like such a short time ago

Chapter 15

since she was a junior secretary and now here, she was in the partner's office having a conversation about another partner.

She didn't see the conversation as a reprimand, which it may have been, but he certainly did seem to want to nip things in the bud if there was a problem and genuinely find out what the problem was.

"Suzanne's time is her own business," said Mr Austin. "I'm just concerned because I need to get the work done regardless of who does it. I know you're a capable young lady that's why I hired you, I just need to know that I didn't make a mistake. "

"Of course not, Mr Austin, it's just that I usually have Suzanne to give me work to do that is required by the partners. Now I must figure out what needs to be done on my own. Not only that but I've had to figure out the client schedules and make sure that the clients are kept happy as well. I'm not sure if Suzanne has her laptop with her or if she's in touch with the clients. I don't think she is.

It's been a rare situation that Irene would have to talk to him, except for the time that she was interviewed by him during her recruitment process.

"Can I be honest with you Mr Austin?" said Irene.

"Go ahead."

"I have some personal problems going on right now. My partner is facing a charge with the criminal authorities, and if you keep this completely confidential, I think Suzanne had something to do with it. I'm sorry but I don't know all the details. I've been doing my best to hold everything together personally and professionally.

"My partner has a daughter who I've been trying to keep in the country because her mother just took her to Spain without my partner's permission.

I've been putting in all the hours and have been doing overtime and I've tried to make sure all the clients have been kept up to date and all their files are uploaded, and everyone is kept happy, and the office is running smoothly but it's hard on your own".

Irene paused for breath and continued.

"I'm glad you called me into the office so that I can have a conversation with you about this. I've been feeling a little isolated to be honest."

"Okay Irene, I appreciate your honesty," the older gentleman said.

Mr Austin appears to believe her after a fashion.

"I had a suspicion something was going on with Suzanne, but I didn't know what, in fact, I still don't but thank you for filling me in. What was she working on the last time she was here, and who is she with?"

"She appeared to be working on the code at a Kouba buildings and she asked me to do some research. I'm not sure if the client meeting ever went ahead at that time", Irene continued. "The client has spoken to me a few times since then, but I'm not sure if he is still on the books or if we lost his business owing to the confusion and the lack of professionalism on our part."

"Since then, I understand, she's taken a leave of absence, informally", said Mr Austin.

"I heard she was at a health spa in the Midlands. Whatever the truth of it is, sir, Suzanne hasn't been around anyway."

Chapter 16

Grace notices that Irene is a little distracted at work and they decide to go and look for Suzanne because she's been missing. Each of them looks in different places, but it turns out that she hasn't been in any of them.

She hasn't been at work. She hasn't been in the tennis club. She hasn't been seen out and about in any of her usual haunts, restaurants, coffee shops, or anything like that.

But one afternoon Irene finds her in the swimming pool they have a discussion. Irene confronts her and notices that she's wearing a designer watch.

Irene begins to question how big a role finance plays in her corporate identities and her personal life. What sacrifices has she made already that were maybe inappropriate for her to make for the sake of financial comfort. She was more worried and restricted.

Suzanne has already made a play for Irene's partner and got him involved in all sorts of problems that he now has to pay for. Irene won't forgive either of them easily. But Gary is certainly the author of his own misfortune, as he went into the problems and the drugs and the cyber-crime of his own volition.

Irene finds out that Suzanne is trying to access the servers of the firm remotely. Thus, she stopped her in her tracks and made sure that she was not able to destroy the evidence, with Rodney's help. Irene decides she is going to learn how to interpret the evidence.

And report Suzanne to the London police to get Gary off the hook. Gary's been sent to prison. And it may be that she can't get him out of prison, but she wants to be sure that Suzanne goes down for her part in this sorry mess.

Behind the scenes Rodney is working on the case because he believes there is more to it. Rodney wants to make sure that the right person is incarcerated. He also wants to see justice served, because he thinks he is beginning to have feelings beyond professionalism for Irene and doesn't want to see her end up with a bad guy.

When Suzanne finally shows her face at the swimming pool. She hadn't been playing tennis as she usually did, and she hadn't been going to work either. In fact, she hadn't been doing much at all except for laying low and trying not to make herself conspicuous. Unfortunately, for her, Irene is there also.

The pool is crowded to begin with. Irene is there first swimming lengths, on the right-hand side nearest the wall. The pool is divided for lane swimming during the hours of six pm to eight pm for serious swimmers only. Learners can only swim outside of these hours. Suzanne shows up at seven thirty pm and starts swimming in the same lane.

This is a common enough occurrence because there are only six lanes and people usually must share, but Irene hadn't seen Suzanne in weeks, and she was absent from the office where they both worked so she was a little shocked to see her sharing the pool, and especially sharing a pool lane.

At eight o'clock precisely, both Suzanne and Irene left the pool, because the juniors we're taking swimming lessons then. The two ladies were barely aware of each other until they each went for a towel on the bench and realised it was the same one. Irene let a little gasp from her open mouth when she realised who was in front of her.

She didn't realise Rodney was at the pool watching everything. He was going to be training juniors in just a moment, but like all good police officers he was constantly on the lookout and absorbing everything in his view.

Suzanne was tall and slim, and it looked like she had taken a sun holiday

Chapter 16

in the meantime, since the last time Irene had spoken to her back at the apartment during that Friday afternoon some time ago.

Irene noticed these things. She was still very affronted by Suzanne and couldn't get over the betrayal which she felt very deeply.

"So, are you going to take my towel as well as my boyfriend," said Irene a little cattily.

"Oh, is this yours? I hadn't realised."

"There are fresh towels available at reception. You just must pay £4.00 for them. They're freshened every day. You can always bring your own. Both suits."

"I'll bear that in mind, thanks."

"So where have you been hanging out these days? Gary's in prison. He could use some support. Well, not exactly prison, but he is in a little bother shall we say. But you knew that, right?"

"Well, I didn't know the details. In fact, I still don't. And honestly, I prefer you didn't speak about my private business in public places like swimming pools. Thank you very much. Are we clear?" Suzanne was still trying to call the shots, and act like she was Irene's boss.

"Perfectly clear Suzanne, but you've no further business telling me what to speak about in public. In fact, I can speak about exactly what I want. You disappeared from the office. You implicated Gary in heavens knows what, and you're in the middle of some drug and business building empire and fake loans scheme!"

"Will you keep your voice down Irene, please?" said Suzanne, getting irate. "You've no business asking me these questions, I have nothing to hide, honestly, I haven't. Have you seen my laptop? I haven't been into the office, and I thought I brought it home with me."

"You know well where it is Suzanne. And you're not getting it. It's going to be in the police hands soon and you're going to go down for a long time for your part in whatever fraud you perpetuated." Irene walks off and into the sauna, livid.

Rodney watched from the sidelines and saw everything, but he couldn't make any move on Suzanne because he wasn't in his police uniform. He was off duty, coaching kids, and he couldn't call for backup. He made a private note in his head that he would find Suzanne and get the evidence to arrest her soon.

Not today, but soon.

Meanwhile, Gary was in prison. And Suzanne had been up to no good. But Irene had been able to stop her in her tracks for the time being. Suzanne was no fool. But neither was Irene, and she had more knowledge about the computers in the office.

Foolishly, Suzanne left her lap-top in the office before disappearing and this might just be her undoing. If Irene can figure out what the pass codes mean in the text file that wasn't encrypted.

The passwords could mean anything, but it most likely wouldn't be anything good.

Irene is full of angst.

She is struggling more with her food issues and is restricting more and getting weaker. In the meantime, she has relinquished the dog regretfully to his owner and she is walking around the block frantically on evenings and mornings on her own instead, counting backwards from one hundred.

She is struggling with her conscience, and she knows she must leave Gary, but she doesn't know how to explain to Rodney that she has feelings for him because things are so complicated.

With the court case and all the things that are being uncovered in it, she feels like Rodney knows too much about her and her life and that's just scary. That's super scary.

Gary had been put away. He was remanded for the final court date in prison. Suzanne was still at large when Irene went to work, and Irene was trying to track down what Suzanne has been up to.

She knew her way around the computer and she found evidence on Suzanne's laptop that linked her to the drug shipment and the cryptocurrency and the stolen loans on properties that existed only virtually.

This appears to be where she got the money from. She must have had a bigger partner because cryptocurrency coins don't come from nowhere. Even Irene knew that. They aren't made from thin air. The money came

Chapter 16

from somewhere.

Even Irene knew that. She had to tip Rodney off that there was something bigger coming down the track.

For the drugs. It seemed like Suzanne was behind it all alone. Gary was a partner in crime, but he was duped into becoming involved.

But she'd been running a squeaky-clean operation.

And the only thing that tied her down was a document with passwords which didn't mean anything. Irene didn't have to decrypt the document itself because it was only on a basic text file. But the passwords seemed to be an encryption key for something that didn't mean anything until she figured it out. And she hadn't yet.

She would have to do this with the help of Rodney.

Luckily for Irene she had a friend inside the real estate firm where she worked. He might be able to help her with the passwords.

When she told Rodney about this, he was quite excited, but cautioned her against asking the friend in the office.

"I insist on taking the laptop, Irene, this is police business," he said. "I know about cyber-crime, and I can lay fresh eyes on this. A police officer's eyes, Irene, don't worry, we'll get Suzanne if she is guilty."

In fact, it was the email that came in from the outside server at the station where he got his tip off in the first place - so he was all for figuring out where this element fits into this puzzle of what is Gary's case. And find out who else is involved.

But this may well be the reason that he gets Suzanne on his radar for the crime that has been committed and maybe he can solve this case once and for all.

Chapter 17

The judge entered the courtroom, where all the benches were wooden and nearly all were occupied by press, interested family members, and the defence and the prosecution. Gary was there with his court appointed lawyer.

A couple of his colleagues from the law office appeared in the public gallery, presumably to find out what was going on and whether it was possible to either dismiss Gary or keep him on, working. The jury would be out on a lot of things, not just whether Gary went to prison.

The room appeared to be a large District Court, as Gary had not been brought to court before, so it was certainly not a High Court. He had been granted station bail after he had made admissions at the police station a few months earlier. But now it was time for the real story to unfold.

Would Gary be able to swing his way out of this one as he had so often in his life before? He recalled his father and how disappointed he had been at the debating competition at university in which he failed (according to his father), which secured his absence from his father's law firm and ensured his brother success.

"All rise," said the judge when he walked into the chambers. "Do we have Mr. Gary Russell in court? And is he represented? Or is he standing for himself? I notice he is a lawyer. Does he have a legal team in place? These are very serious charges, you realise this, Mr Russell?"

Chapter 17

Gary is a bit startled to hear himself being referred to in the third person, and he pauses for a second to take a breath. He takes in the surroundings of the wooden chambers, the judge in his black robes and headdress. He shudders.

"I do, your honour," said Gary, after a pause.

"You can speed it up there a little, now. We don't have all day," said the judge. Can you state your name for the record?"

"Gary Russell, your honour."

"And the legal team of the defence. Can you please name yourselves?"

"Neil Skater, judge. I'm Mr Russell's legal counsel."

"Do you have copies of all the charges? Do you understand all the charges against you? And how are you pleading?"

"Not guilty your honour", said Gary.

The judge motioned for the police constable to speak. "What are the charges, and do you have evidence?"

"Your honour, we've reached a plea in relation to the drug charges, he said. They are to be struck out, as they have been fully investigated and found to be without foundation. However, during the investigation, we uncovered a serious crime in relation to fraud."

"That should be struck out also," interjected Neil Skater. "The interview with my client was taking place under duress and the only reason my client was being interviewed was in relation to the drugs charge which were found to be spurious."

"Drug charges" said the judge, raising an eyebrow over his bifocal glasses. "That's interesting. I'll hear the evidence."

"Can we adjourn for a moment, your honour? I'd like to approach the bench,"

"I'll allow it."

It was the defendant's lawyer Neil Skater who spoke, and he noticed that the prosecution lawyer was a man he went to law school with - three lawyers, including Gary, and one judge, all of whom appeared to know the law inside out.

This could either be good for Gary or bad, depending on what the relationship was like between all of the men. Or what mood the judge happened to be in on the day. He tried to get a sense of the judge earlier, but he was obviously mistaken that they would take the plea as read.

What would happen for Gary.

Guilty or not guilty. Free to go, or not. Either way, the outcome for Gary was likely to be grim. If he was free to go, he appeared not to have the confidence of his employers anymore and was out of a job. If he wasn't free to go, he was in jail.

So, what was to be done? The required minimum, according to the judge, was to hear the evidence. Now that the drug habit and various matters were being investigated in terms of possession and in terms of dealing and receiving shipments, well, it could be all over for him. Truly it could.

"Back to the matter at hand," said the judge.

"You attended the interview, Mr Skater. If you had a problem with the way the interview was going, you should have said it back then," said the prosecuting counsel. Your client was duly arrested and questioned on suspicion of an offence."

"Yes, I understand counsel, but anything that was uncovered during an illegal interview can't be taken seriously and used as evidence. You know that."

"I'll decide that!" retorted the judge. "You don't get to make those decisions Counsel".

"This should have been sorted out before you got to the chamber gentlemen," said the judge. "No conversations in my courtroom, not between the trial prosecution and the defence team."

"How are we to continue now?" Gary's lawyer looked forlorn.

"Prosecution, do you have a book of evidence to present to court? The only question for me now is whether the evidence was obtained lawfully, and whether it should be put to a jury."

Meanwhile, back at the office Irene was in another world. For Irene, the jury was out on whether he had done it or not, and she doesn't know what to believe. The drug charges were now off the table, she thought. But the white-collar crime was not a good look for her. It was bad for her career and

Chapter 17

personal life on so many levels. Could she really forgive him? What about Rosie, how could she help bring her back to London? And why would she want to? Maybe Rosie and Julia were better off in Spain, without Gary.

Suddenly, she decided to go to the courtroom to meet Gary and to find out what was going on. It was nearly five o'clock anyway and she had finished her work for the day as she usually did. She had never been to the courthouse, but she had some idea of police procedure having watched it on television so often. Yes, that sounded like a good plan.

Irene's mum called her out of the blue, just as she was leaving the office to head to the court.

She wanted to have a private video call conversation that couldn't wait. Turns out she had something important to say.

"It'll only take five minutes," said her mum. "I've had to get my nerve up to have this call with you and I must tell you something. It can't wait any longer."

"Spit it out mum if it's something important, just get it over with."

"You've got family in Ireland that I never told you about."

Chapter 18

It turns out Irene was adopted at birth and never told the story of what happened.

"We chose you because we thought we couldn't have kids of our own and at the time, it was an easy possibility because the family we took you from couldn't take care of you at the time. You know, I've always been fond of Ireland. Well, that's the truth. It was an unexpected event. Nobody plans for these things. Certainly, we didn't all those years ago when you were born. Do you have anything to say Irene?"

Irene was shocked that her mom would bring this up now. She really didn't know what to say at this stage. She had nearly forgotten that her mom told her about the adoption when she was a child, because it certainly wasn't mentioned again.

She didn't know who knew, and she never gave it much head space. She never told anyone about it, and she must have buried the memory, because it seemed that now she might be forced to deal with the issue as an adult and make decisions she had forgotten she may have to make at some point in the future. It certainly wasn't ideal.

Irene was still on the phone on her video call to her mum and she could see her in the living room at their family home where she had lived her whole childhood.

She was about to say something, but bit her lip and refrained, and she

Chapter 18

realised that she really didn't have any cause to complain about her upbringing. It must have been hard for her mum to make a call like this, and she was sure she didn't do it lightly.

"So why are you telling me now?" asked Irene, forgetting about the plan to go to the court house. Her mum could have let it slide, but suddenly Irene feels an uncontrollable urge to know who her birth mum and dad were.

The woman who gave birth to her. Was there a relationship in the picture, or was it an uncomfortable story of some sordid affair? Why did she need to give away her baby?

"Has there been any contact over the years, mum, I'd like to know?" asked Irene quietly after a brief pause.

"Well, yes, there were a few letters and cards that were sent in the first few years of her life that you have never seen. If you come home, I'll show them to you."

And this was hard for Irene to hear, that her birth mom would have sent cards.

"Oh, mum, I wish you would have told me this sooner."

She's deciding momentarily that her mother may want the same thing – to get in touch and see if they could get to know each other - but she knows how good her parents were to her, so she doesn't want to hurt them.

But she also knew that she would track down her birth family one way or the other in the not-too-distant future, but now she just had to park that idea.

Irene noticed suddenly as she stroked her own neck in an un-selfconscious movement of comfort and self-care, that she was wearing several necklaces at the same time.

And she thought that this might stand for her different psychological states and now her different families. She is conflicted and confused and needs some tender loving care.

Who can she get that from, except herself?

At this point, Irene questioned her motives for continuing in the relationship with Gary at all, and she considered perhaps that the only reason she stuck with him is for the sake of the fact that they have a mortgage on an apartment together.

Meanwhile, her heart skips a beat when she thinks of Rodney and wonders what it would be like to be with him.

And she wonders, is this good enough?

A brief attack of panic happens to Irene where she considers she must be a moral failure if that is the case, that she's so shallow that she can be worried about the mortgage rather than her sanity or her sense of conscience and good ethics.

She feels nauseous on the underground and she must make a quick exit. She wipes her mouth and brushes her teeth with the toothbrush she carries for emergencies.

She knows Gary has done wrong and she needs to park that for the moment to deal with the issues that are at hand.

Irene, longs for a little tenderness, and she has been thinking about Rodney more and more lately. She wonders if it's the same for him.

And insofar as her attitude to her relationship has changed, her attitude to life has become more serious.

She has developed a moral compass, had a brief wobble, and now she's found it again. She was a little self-absorbed, but now she seems to be a bit more circumspect.

Chapter 19

Irene got a phone call the next week from her mother, asking for a visit as her dad's been unwell. They lived in a small suburb of London an hour away on the tube, and Irene doesn't drive, so she set out one Saturday on the train to visit for the weekend. She carried a small backpack because she planned to stay for a few days and have that much needed break that she'd been planning. She listened to her iPod with her favourite music on the train and relaxes.

"Your dad's been poorly," said Irene's mom, on the phone when she called. "He had a heart attack, but I didn't tell you as I didn't want to worry you. I know you've been going through so much stress. And I know you suffer from anxiety the same as your dad does."

"Yes, of course I'll come home, mum," said Irene, worriedly. Just give me until the end of the week, is he in hospital?

"No, thankfully he's not in the hospital. Of course, the end of the week is fine, he was in hospital earlier. But he's home now and he's asking for you."

"Okay, Mum. Is there anything else I can do?

Can I bring anything from London with me that he might like?"

"No, just bring yourself. He'll be happy with that, and your sister will be happy to see you too. And me of course."

And with that, they ended the telephone conversation. She hadn't told her mom about Gary, the court case or anything else for that matter that she was going through now.

There would be time for that later, or maybe there wouldn't.

Irene was very protective of her younger sister, who was at a local college doing her A levels, and she loved to see her as much as possible.

She had bought her laptop for her Christmas present the previous year and she wondered how it was helping her with her studies now.

One thing is for sure, she wouldn't be able to afford to pay for a laptop for her present now, with the situation about her finances as they were.

There it was again, the elephant in the room. Gary in prison. Unable to contribute to the mortgage and bills.

Irene's Mom waits until she is there. Before she comes clean about the rest of the details about the adoption, they have been upfront all along about the fact that she was adopted, but the details surrounding the adoption have been sketchy up until now.

She's been told on the last video call with her mom that she came from Ireland at six months of age. Turns out she came from a wealthy family who ran a hotel and businesses in the west of Ireland.

The only reason she was adopted was because her mom was single and estranged from the family due to her pregnancy and she was a premature baby, so she wasn't thought to live long. The couple, Irene's parents who adopted her, were staying at the hotel at the time and decided to take her when the opportunity arose.

They had thought that they weren't able to have children and they were sorry they hadn't told her sooner.

Her mom said to Irene, I'm sorry I didn't come clean about it sooner, but it was an adoption that wasn't done through the proper channels, and we were embarrassed. I know it wasn't the right thing to do. But both your dad and I wanted to do right by you as soon as we saw you. You were taken out of the hospital at six months old, but you looked only two months old.

You were under-weight and you looked so poorly.

Your mother was a 17-year-old schoolchild who would have been kicked out of her family had she not given up her daughter. It was very difficult to think about then. It was a horrifically hard situation.

Chapter 19

Irene's mom thought of her birth mom's situation, and they made the best of it, but they never stayed in touch, not after the first couple of letters and cards. Irene's mom didn't reply, and her mother stopped writing.

After that, Irene's parents were too afraid to go back to Ireland in case someone would find out about the situation and try to take her away.

Irene decided then and there, once she found out that she was going to go off and look for her birth mom. She would still be young and who knows maybe they'd form a deep relationship and she'd find out all the missing pieces about her life and why she was the way she was. She'd find out if she looked like anybody or sounded like anybody or had the same talents as anybody else. She wondered if she had any siblings in Ireland.

She really didn't know what to think. But she couldn't think badly of her parents. Because they had done a good job with her and given her a decent life.

But it sure was bad timing, she thought, as her head spun out of control with all that was going on for her right now.

Chapter 20

Irene and her dad have a conversation while he's on his deathbed, and she makes a pact with him.

That she will always look after her mother and her sister, but she also says that she must look after her own needs to find out who her birth mum is and track her down in Ireland.

She's going to go and look for her. Irene's dad understands, but he's weak and on life support at this stage, so when the nurse comes in and tells Irene that it's over, that her dad isn't coming back, she's devastated.

She barely knows or remembers if he knew that she was there at the time or if he could understand the conversation that she was asking him to have.

She's traumatized but is determined to be there for her mom and sister like she promised her dad she would.

Oh, she wished Rodney could be there, and decided to text him later just to say hello. She'd like him to know that she was there that she was thinking about him even if he doesn't know why she needs it so much.

The understanding she made with her dad on his deathbed led to even more trauma and drama for her when he died. She was there for her mother for two weeks and was still away from the scene in London.

Behind the scenes, Rodney was working on the case, among other things.

Chapter 20

He was also busy with his brother and the swim team, and he noticed that Irene wasn't there and hasn't been for a while. He was delighted to get her text and Rodney calls her back to find out if she was okay, and she told him she was, but thanked him for checking up on her.

Gary works on his appeal, but his legal team is costing him a lot, as even in London for a lawyer he doesn't seem to be able to pull any favours.

Suzanne is trying to stay out of prison, but she knows that everything's closing in on her.

Rodney was on the brink of solving the case of Suzanne and the missing Cryptocurrency, but he still hasn't found the drugs stashed in the tennis club and he didn't know about them yet. That could be a situation that could be very difficult for Gary to explain.

And it could be the reason he would go away for good.

Rodney pops up in his bicycle shorts and faded jeans and swim shorts in Irene's imagination, but this is just fantasy.

Irene's thoughts go to the circumstances that have led her down this path so many times before, which have dragged her in and out of dodgy relationships and hospitals and oh, she's fed-up thinking.

She allows the thoughts to go from her mind.

She finds it difficult but she's using a new brain training technique that helps while she grabs her coat and walks out the door. You count aloud one, two, three, four, five, and then again, one, two, three, four, five and backwards, five, four, three, two, one, while you're walking.

Eventually, you will stop thinking about whatever has been on your mind that has preoccupied you unnecessarily.

If this doesn't work, you start counting backwards from one hundred. One hundred, ninety-nine, ninety-eight, ninety-seven, ninety-six. Irene found it worked, and when she became obsessive in her thinking, it alleviated the problem for a little while.

Sergeant Moran, on the other hand, knew that Gary was guilty.

He knew about the drugs.

He hasn't quite made the exact connection with Suzanne, but he knows she's guilty too. He just needs proof and he's got to ensure Irene is the one to give it to them. How can he engineer another meeting with Irene where her guard is fully down?

The interview at the station gave him some of the information he needed, but he knew Irene was holding something back, he suspected anyway.

When Moran found a lead on Suzanne, he left the station without his glasses and nearly caused an accident while driving without them. That one would be hard to explain to his superiors!

Irene was devastated when her dad died. She was there for two weeks following the funeral to look after her mum, and during that time, she has a lot of time to think.

She was still thinking about Gary and whether she should continue with him, or start afresh, and go to Ireland to find her family. She can start to look for them first by doing some investigative work, online or in libraries, or even by asking her mum if she has any information.

She'd already found out that the adoption wasn't exactly legal, so it may well be difficult to find out the information given the passage of so much time. Twenty-five years was a long time for Irene, a lifetime in fact.

It was some admission for her mum to make. But maybe her mum just didn't know the full story about her birth mother. And maybe her memories are a little bit skewed with the passage of so much time.

Before long she's called back to London but not before she sees her dad's grave again and gets a chance to say goodbye.

There was a will reading and it turns out her father wanted Irene to have an inheritance of some money and a small apartment in Andalusia in Spain.

She didn't even know that he had an apartment in Spain!

She at once thought that the money would tide her over for a while to decide what it is she wanted to do.

It will give her some choices that she really didn't think she had. She didn't know what she wanted yet.

And it was high time she found out.

Chapter 21

With Irene back in London, everything was on top of her, and her racing thoughts and anxiety was back with a vengeance. She was still not eating properly and she was exercising all the time. She was getting weaker, but she felt it was the only way she could stay in control.

Gary was still in prison, which in one way was a blessing in disguise, as she was learning to live without him, but in another it's quite difficult for her.

After the unexpected phone call from Julia in Spain about Rosie having leukaemia, she was devastated, and this is just adding to her woes. This is the news every mum and dad dreads. And every step mum. With her own anxiety and her dad's illness, death, and now the possibility that Rosie has a childhood cancer, it was all getting too much for her.

Grace, her friend from accounts in the office, was usually her advocate when it comes to her health. And Grace recommended visiting her doctor and coming clean about everything that had been going on.

"In fairness Irene," said Grace, one morning when she stopped by Irene's desk with coffee and a donut.

Irene refused the donut.

"You haven't seen him in ages, and you haven't been yourself lately. If I'm not mistaken, you've started vaping electronic cigarettes again! And you just don't look like yourself. I'm worried about you."

Without much objection, Irene agrees. She hasn't started smoking. It's just that she's not looking after herself as well as she used to, and her appearance is not up to its usual standard.

Later, the conversation with the doctor wasn't pleasant, as he realises, she appears not to have been eating regularly either.

Drinking coffee and over-exercising had become a regular habit to keep her going through the day. And it gave her some control. She gave up smoking in recent times, she used to find it helps her relax.

She knew it was no solution to her problems, but she had been thinking of going back to it, lately.

How horrible, she thought.

Her doctor notices that she appears to have lost more weight.

"Overexercising is bad for anyone. Especially someone with your history, Irene," the doctor ventured, looking for more information.

Although she hasn't been exercising or swimming since the episode at the pool with Suzanne, the overexercising by walking everywhere possibly started when she took in the stray dog from the shelter and hadn't stopped when she gave the dog back to its owner.

She had lost muscle mass since the last time the doctor checked.

Upon further probing, Irene said she hasn't been concerned about eating regularly. Or over-exercising for that matter. She wasn't self-aware at that moment of her condition, or how it may escalate.

This was what the doctor is worried about.

Irene had just lost her father and because she presented at the doctor's office, it was a scary time for her, and he was worried about her.

This is something she had a problem with when she was in her two-year diploma programme, and it's one of the reasons she exited before getting a four-year degree.

But it's a warm, happy place, hospital, she remembered. With warm, happy people. An eclectic mix.

There's a private room with an en-suite shower and regular mealtimes that you don't have to cook for yourself, which are formulated just for your needs.

Chapter 21

The nurses and doctors are lovely and really, she has no complaints.

The patients at the hospital could be a little problematic sometimes if Irene was honest. If maybe they asked the wrong question, and she was feeling a little vulnerable, and maybe they weren't as politically correct as she might be. That could be awkward, but generally everything was fine.

Irene was still worried she wouldn't be able to pay her mortgage. She was worried about this for the first few days she was in hospital, and she couldn't relax.

She didn't have any access to the outside world because her phone was taken away.

This was so she could really switch off, as she appeared to be a little hyper and unsettled.

But the more she took part in the social aspect of the groups at hospital and spoke to the social workers, she began to realise that maybe her job and all those things that she had worked so hard for in London maybe, her life needs re-evaluating.

She thinks about this on her own, after a few therapy sessions and quiet room sessions. After a group. And after a chat with some of the other folks who have been through this for longer, she begins to draw conclusions that her own life needs changing.

But she's still not sure what she needs to do.

The hospital doctor who attended to her and the nurses say should be able to get better and she just needed to rest and recover for a week or 10 days, she would be helped.

She would be able to get back to her normal life.

She was just not sure what normal life is anymore.

Maybe she wanted a new normal.

Maybe, just maybe, there was more to life than mortgages in London and real estate companies.

And white-collar criminals for a partner and boss. Maybe she found this out before, when she was in college and going out with the other man who left her the last time she was suffering from anxiety.

He didn't understand and he didn't want to understand. She wondered why she stuck it out with Gary for so long. And now she was wondering how she got herself so tied up in his life.

She was in danger of overthinking things. So, she was happy when Grace came to visit after dinner one evening.

It was a distraction from all the private thinking she did in the hospital.

She hadn't had too much contact with Grace since the office because they were mainly colleagues who worked together, but Grace would come to visit and she was a great help.

Grace's visit came after one week, and it was very welcome, she brought flowers. They played a great game of Scrabble together and they watched a soap opera on the TV in the visitor's room.

Irene was happy because she got a triple word score on only the third turn and Grace let her win in the end. At least it seemed that way, Irene wasn't sure.

Rodney came by and brought her a card and one of the smoothies she likes. He really went above and beyond the call of duty, Irene thinks, but she's happy, nonetheless. She is beginning to warm to him.

She doesn't think it's a bit creepy that he remembers what kind of smoothie she likes and takes it in the spirit in which she thinks it is intended, a gesture of friendship and care for someone who hasn't been eating properly. Someone he would like to know better.

Gary's still in prison, but she can make a call to him the occasional time by arrangement. She's devastated at the idea that Rosie has leukaemia, but she needed to get better herself and work on her own issues.

Irene realises before long she will have problems to face when she goes back to work and at some stage, she concludes that she will not go back to work at the real estate agency, and she will quit her job and get something else.

This causes her a great deal of angst, but it's only a job after all, and she is only twenty-five years old, she realises suddenly. She still had a lot of living to do yet.

In some respects, she feels like an old woman, with so many responsibilities, and in other ways she feels like leaving it all behind.

Chapter 21

She didn't come to this conclusion at once. In fact, she didn't come to it on her own at all. She came to this conclusion after a phone call from Mr Austin, the real estate partner, and after a great deal of reflection on her part.

"So, Irene," Mr Austin said, in a phone call to her after she was allowed to get her phone back the second week. "When are you coming back to work? We really could use your help, especially with Suzanne still gone."

"With all due respect Mr Austin, Suzanne isn't my problem. I need to look after myself. I am in hospital; you do realise that."

"Of course, I realised that Irene, it's no harm to ask. I just wanted to make sure you were alright. I didn't want to visit without asking or without contacting you first."

"Oh, that's very kind Mr Austin, but really there's no need. Honestly, I'm in the best place and I'm getting the care I need, and I'll be in touch as soon as I can."

"But, Irene, can you give me some kind of a time frame? Any kind at all for when you might be back. We are still paying you after all."

"I'm not sure of the finer details of my contract, Mr Austin, but I'm sure whatever benefits I get in terms of pay is in line with industry standards and norms." Suddenly she felt bold again and liberated as she spoke.

Irene realises suddenly they don't appear in the firm to have any understanding of what her problem is, or her needs are, or maybe they were being passive aggressive.

On one level she knows Mr Austin is right to remark that they can't keep paying her forever, but it's only been three weeks that she's been in hospital. And that doesn't seem like a lot.

And now she felt like she can't go back. She was feeling a little exposed for sure. It's not that she thought they're bad employers, she just realised the whole financial system in London may not be exactly what she thought it was going to be, and she felt like quitting - she just wanted out.

And that apartment in Andalusia, well, it needed visiting. She would love to find out what her father wanted her to have in terms of a legacy.

Also, she had family in Ireland that she wanted to look up and contact. She buys a book about adoption in the hospital book shop and reads it over the course of a weekend, to find out the best way to approach a birth family.

One day, the previous week, a new patient came into the ward and said hello to her. She responded back with a muted greeting.

It was quite difficult to get people to speak here, and often, she only got to speak to the nurses once in the morning when they checked her blood pressure. The patients were friendly enough over meals, but they were all here for their own reasons, and basically the only work she can get done is in the therapy sessions and support groups.

That's when the real work is done. There are learning opportunities, and a library so she can read books in her downtime. When she is not thinking about her problems or dealing with a visitor or nurse or doctor.

And Irene begins to question her whole lifestyle choices. The swimming, the gluten free diet, the exercise, the job, Gary.

Gary. She spoke his name aloud in her head.

Her commitment to continue living in the apartment with Gary, and suddenly realised her world was built on a lie, a world based on sand.

It was a house with no foundation and she wants to find a way out. She attends therapy at the hospital, and she tried to get back to her regular eating.

"I'm quitting smoking again," she says one day, for she had started again in hospital, and she does.

Irene made friends, she makes a friend at the hospital, the one who came in and said hello and asked if she was going to take her own life and Irene said no, she had just come into hospital for a rest.

And so, after that Irene made the decision that she would quit her job and she does, but the question then is, how is she going to pay for her apartment and continue to pay her bills.

One day before she leaves hospital for the last time, Julia comes to visit unexpectedly.

She's back in London and Rosie is attending a hospital nearby, paid for by Gary's National Health Insurance. Julia knows he can't get private treatment as she has had sight of his finances.

But she knows she will get better treatment in London than in her small coastal village on the Costa Blanca in Spain where she is nowhere near a

Chapter 21

hospital.

Julia is very worried about her daughter but has also missed London. It had felt like she was taking a step backwards in time in Spain, she confided in Irene over a coffee in the hospital canteen.

The leukaemia treatment which Rosie is currently going through is compounding all Julia's problems such as the need to work and find suitable living space again.

Irene likes Julia but she doesn't feel like confiding in her about her problems. Julia is certainly taking advantage of her Irene's listening ear right now and telling her all about hers. Julia's problems are all about being poor and not having a job or money for rent or a college education.

Irene doesn't share her problems.

There's only one thing she did know and that was that her problems are very different to Julia's, but they do share Rosie in common, but for how long?

Gary and the connectedness they used to share were very much off Irene's radar now, and she has emotionally checked out of the relationship with him.

Irene is surprised at how much Julia is willing to share about her problems, but she has realised for a while that Julia has been isolated and alone. She hadn't realised until then, until this visit to the hospital, just how isolated she had become too. A whole new change was upon her, and she didn't know what the future held in store.

"Do you think maybe when this is all over, we can become friends?" Julia said suddenly.

"I don't know, maybe," said Irene. "I thought we were friends already, it's not all about Gary, you know."

Both women have dealt with loss and suffering recently and the future looms large for each of them financially.

Julia's maintenance was based on Gary's job and ability to keep her, and she felt unable to work herself regularly enough to keep Rosie and herself in London. Of course, if you can't get a job, it's hard. And it wasn't as easy for someone to live a good lifestyle and look after a sick child as well as keep a job and a roof over their head.

Irene must face challenges too now, and she's got obstacles. But she's in a good place to face them. Emotionally anyway.

But she's decided to quit her job and she has already sent the final email to her boss. It hasn't been responded to, but it may well be in due course. It wasn't a formal resignation, just a request for more time.

She now faced the prospect of losing her London home because she couldn't share it with Gary anymore. She had bittersweet thoughts about her dad and the Andalusia apartment that she had yet to see.

There was no question of keeping the London apartment, they must sell. So, she must think about going back to live with her mum.

So that might be what would happen, she thinks anyway. It appeared that all of this has been just going on in her head for ages and ages. But really, it had only been three weeks.

The full length of time that she's been in hospital. And maybe a little bit prior to that she's not sure how long. But certainly, she'd been fragile for a while.

In the end, Irene checks herself out after three weeks, as she doesn't want to cause any more pain to her family, and she does have responsibilities, which she is dealing with.

Chapter 22

It turns out Suzanne had been in a rented apartment in Scotland. She had also been trying to sort out her chequered history of police problems and evading capture. But this could only work for so long. The long arm of the law would soon stretch to where she happens to be.

Suzanne would soon tell all manner of lies to the police to keep Gary in prison and to get herself out.

Gary got hold of her on the phone one day and found out where she was, as she hadn't covered her tracks well enough and had not abandoned her phone or email address.

Rodney had been doing some investigating on Suzanne and he figured out that she was having a longstanding affair with Gary. If she wasn't having an affair with him, why did she ring him 168 times in six weeks?

The affair might explain their feelings and why they were texting and calling so many times. In addition, the fact that the drugs arrived in the country on a shipping container on a particular morning.

There were the admissions about the planning applications and mortgages coupled with the cryptocurrency.

Well, you didn't need to be a genius.

Rodney eventually tracked her down in a bed and breakfast in Glasgow following an intercepted telephone call between herself and Gary.

It was amazing how many criminal deals were done over a telephone call in dodgy hotels from cities just outside the jurisdiction, Rodney thought to himself, smugly, as he thought how he would catch Suzanne and get the proof he needed to make sure she went away for a long time.

Meanwhile, Gary rings her from the police station when he's got permission to make a phone call. And unfortunately for her she answers, and it appears that the phones are being surveilled in the prison. She incriminates herself at once just knowing his telephone number and that he was in prison.

"Hi Gary," she says, cheerily.

"Hi, Suzanne, he says, not so cheerily. How's life where you are? And what have you been up to?"

"Oh, up I'm up north in Scotland and I haven't been in touch, I'm so sorry. What happened with you? What did that police officer want in the end? Was it your TV licence or something?", Suzanne lied.

"Don't come the innocent with me, Suzanne. Really, I don't want you playing any games. The time for games is over, you need to make admissions to the police about what kind of deal was going on. Please. I must get out of here. I'm not taking all the rap on my own."

"What sort of admissions are you talking about? I'm not about to incriminate myself in any dealings if that's what you mean.

"Oh Suzanne, dear sweet Suzanne. You will make admissions. You will tell the truth, because I know you were scamming me, just as surely as you were scamming that company of yours."

"I don't know what you're talking about, Gary. There was a legitimate business deal, you got paid, I got paid, the deal got done, that's it. If you weren't quick enough to get your money out, that's on you. Or if you gambled it like the loser, you are, that's also on you. But as for any drug dealing, I don't know anything about that."

"I don't either. That's the thing. If you're still out, can you get something out of the tennis club for me? In the fourth locker from the left on the wall, the code is nine-five-four-three-seven. Can you get what's in there and destroy it for me?

Please Suzanne if I ever meant anything to you. Just do this for me. It's just a small package of what came in from the shipment, but I'll never get out of

Chapter 22

jail if I'm connected to it."

"Oh Gary, I didn't know you were that stupid. I'm not going to remove your stash, that's what the police officers had on you when they went to your house, isn't it? So, what exactly do you think is going on here? That we're in this together? Don't make me laugh. And why are you still in jail? Can you not get out of it? Are you the lawyer?"

"No, I've got counsel and he's giving me advice, but there will be a court case that's for sure. And you will be arrested too, it's only a matter of time, you were at the apartment too, only you skipped out as soon as you saw the police officers. That was smart of you. Did you set that whole thing up so that Irene would find us together?"

"Oh, get over yourself, Gary. You're not that special. I don't know what I ever saw in you. Irene had a lucky escape from what I can see."

Meanwhile, in an office in Scotland Yard, a junior police officer listened to the live telephone call that he intercepted and planned for the arrest of Suzanne Barron. He traces her computer address to an hotel in Glasgow and waits.

In a final showdown, just as she had been planning to drive onto a car-ferry, Suzanne was arrested.

Her car was seized, and she was brought to the station for questioning on the charges in relation to the commercial property. She now had a new laptop and phone, and they were also taken. She appeared to have known she couldn't get away with any more of this criminality, and her days were numbered.

Her escape plan didn't go the way she hoped, however, and she was nabbed!

Chapter 23

Irene and Julia have come to an understanding. They've agreed to be friends, and Irene has asked to see Rosie in the children's hospital at Great Ormond Street. When Irene visits, she is told to wear a white sterile overcoat so that she doesn't bring any infection into the ward.

"Are you being brave for the doctors and nurses and your mum?" Irene asks the girl when she gets to her bedside.

Rosie answers back quietly, but firmly.

"Yes of course, but I hate this treatment, I really hate being sick. I want to go home!"

"I'm sure you do Rosie, but it'll all be over soon, I'm sure you'll be home in no time."

Irene is so weak physically and emotionally that she still can't eat, and she's admitted to hospital unexpectedly one day after another referral from her doctor. Again. This is the second admission in two months! She's devastated to be in again and she really thinks she might never recover.

She's still devastated about her dad dying and all the things she never got to say to him living away from home for the last few years she hadn't been as close to him as she wanted to be, and as she once was.

She's never been sure how her sister was going to react when she finds

Chapter 23

out she's been in hospital. She's fragile too. She has the same problem. She has always thought it was in the genes and she wondered if her sister was adopted as well? If they had that blood connection. Or why she had the affinity for her sister that she always had. Irene had a big heart, she had room for a lot of people in it. Still, she was not sure why she bought her sister a laptop for college course, not even knowing if her sister was going to finish. She certainly wanted to encourage her.

Last Christmas, it cost £600. But she knew this year she wouldn't be able to buy anything like that with all the bills she had and the problems with Gary, of course and his family and his ex and, oh, it was all a mess. She thought of trying to get an advance on her salary.

But when she found Mr. Austin, she found him still wondering when she was coming back to work, and he was less than supportive. As an older partner, he was not used to human resources matters.

When she questioned him on why he wouldn't have a policy on sick leave that was supportive of employees, he was less than supportive.

"Your emotional health is your own business, Irene. I just need to know when my work is going to get done. We're a small business here that needs to run while Suzanne and you are away," he said.

"I don't know when she'll be back, truly I don't, all I know is I need a little time, but if you're not prepared to give it to me, then that's fine, I'll hand in my notice."

She suddenly remembered the money her dad had left her, and the Spanish apartment, so she figured she could sort something out until the money came through probate. Yes, that was what she'd do, she'd sort something out, but she knew now that she needed to leave London and sell the apartment and uncouple from Gary was exactly what she needed.

Once Gary realized that he could win his appeal and Irene realized that she could take control of her own life, things got easier, and they both planned separately to overcome the problems that have caused them to be where they are.

Gary wonders what his long-term consequences career wise will be because he's a lawyer and he has been in prison, so he will be struck off the lawyers register, which often leads to major problems, not to mention debt and bills.

Irene came to the decision that her career choice may not be aligned with her core values at all. Secretarial work at a real estate agency could be soulless in the end, and she needed something that was more value-laden, and that fulfilled her more. She needed to find her reason for working, it couldn't just be to get a paycheck, could it?

Meanwhile, back in London, Suzanne was still behind bars, and it looked like they're going to throw away the key for her because it turned out that her scheme has been bigger and bigger, and it was linked to more buildings across London and not just the one building that was originally thought to have involved Gary.

The police put out a televised appeal for more information on the case to solidify their evidence. There were more people involved and Constable Rodney and the Inspector have been busy trying to get to the bottom of this, but they have not yet succeeded

Irene tells Rodney about the time she caught Suzanne trying to clear evidence on the computer by logging in remotely and destroying files.

Rodney examined the computer and shrieked when he found all the evidence which may have locked her away. He figures out what the text file means and how it is linked to the evidence of the planning application, and more.

This new evidence may be what was needed to potentially release Gary to be with his family. Gary had now lost face and his career would certainly be damaged for some time, but he may yet get it back.

Irene finally confides in her mum about the breakup with Gary. As she has been keeping the difficulties under wraps until now and only really talking to Grace from the office, she knows this hasn't been the right thing to do, but she just hasn't felt able to speak to her mum.

Not since the conversation and revelations about the facts of the adoption, which she didn't have that much of an idea about until recently.

It's not that their relationship is strained. It's not.

It's just that she's in the wrong head space to deal with her family right now when she wants to look for her birth family in Ireland.

Chapter 23

Her mum chastises her about Gary when she finds they have broken up and finds she is selling the apartment. Embarrassed, Irene doesn't say why they have broken up.

"Irene you you're never going to get a husband, if you keep turning down proposals, he would have married you by now and then you wouldn't have this problem. I'm no major fan of Gary, I don't know what he's like. Only you do. But I do know that you've brought these problems on yourself. Certainly. You have it all!"

"You really think so, Mum? I can't imagine why you think that. He was doing the wrong thing all along! That's just all I have to say about it. That's just it. I'm leaving him. Some people change, but most people don't. And that's it. I'm leaving. I haven't told you the whole story and I don't want to and to truthful I might be leaving London too."

"Leaving London?" Her mother was horrified. "But your whole life is here! Why ever would you want to leave, Irene?"

"Oh Mum. I'm sorry. But the whole business with the adoption. I can't believe you didn't tell me the whole story. I mean I'm looking back through my life and all the significant portions of it. And it all seems to boil down to one significant thing that happened that I didn't know about. And when I think of that, I think of all the other significant things that I may not have been told about that I may not remember about. Is there anything else you're keeping from me?"

"Oh, Irene! Where did this anger come from? You say you're sorry! You sure don't sound like it. I'm sorry I didn't tell you."

"Really, I don't know for sure yet, Mum. But I do think so, yes. Gary and I are finished. Yes, I'll probably sell the Spanish apartment. I'll sell the apartment in London. And start fresh somewhere else."

"It doesn't mean I don't love you, Mum. But I need to start somewhere else, I need to go back to Ireland, where I was born and track down my birth parents if I can."

"I must ask you, and I'm sorry if it hurts, but can you remember the name of the hotel they used to run? Or their name?"

"Yes Irene. Your mum's name was Ciara Finnegan, and she would be forty-two by now, as she was seventeen when you were born. I've never forgotten about her and what she had to give up. The hotel was on the Atlantic Seaboard not far from Galway city. Go Irene. Go and find her, with my blessing."

Chapter 24

There was mention of a financial reward from the affected real estate company for the illegal activity which was uncovered by Suzanne. Irene ended up getting it. She has shown bravery and courage uncovering the truth.

It's not that much money, but it will at least tide her over for a few months until she decides what to do. And the inherited gift of a sum of money and a small Spanish apartment from her father who wanted her to have something solid as a financial backing in case of his early demise will come to fruition soon as probate clears.

In the end she decides to move in with Grace for a while. She has always wanted to travel more, so she may do that. She hopes to go to Spain to visit her father's apartment, and to visit the hotel on the Atlantic seaboard in Ireland in search of her mother. Who knows what she may have found?

Irene started making voice notes on her phone about how her day was going because she really didn't have anyone else to talk to.

Rodney is not there all the time, although he does text her at least once a day and calls as often as he can.

She still hasn't figured out a way to make him an ally in any real way. Maybe she's just used to a more in-depth type of relationship, but she fancies him certainly, those blue eyes and yeah, yes, well she makes voice notes, and she wonders why.

Nobody hears. Nobody hears her darkest desires.

Not now. For ages, nobody had asked about her health. She always asked after theirs and she's always nice and polite, and yet, she's not quite sure anybody cares. She just ended up again in a relationship where she was downtrodden and taken for granted, the same way it was before when she was in college.

She had to figure out a way to get over the limiting beliefs that held her back in life, and she felt like it was that way it was working as well, with Mr. Austin and the other partners at the firm.

Have some pizza, she thought, *because she hadn't eaten in a few hours.*

Julia and Irene talk, and they come to an understanding they have both had kind of complicated relationships with Gary. Especially with Rosie in the middle, Irene tried to broach the subject of whether Julia would like to get back together romantically with Gary.

She had been thinking about them as a family unit for a while now and can see they might deserve each other in a way that she might not have thought of before.

She doesn't have regrets about Gary as such, but their relationship wasn't as long standing as his and Julia's, and she just wants to know what Julia's thoughts are.

There is one thing she knows for sure; Irene is done with Gary anyway. She's changed and grown and moved on, and now she just needs to buy the tee-shirt and wear it!

Irene had helped Rodney enormously on the case but it was time for her to work on herself now.

She moved out of the London apartment just as it was being sold. This is very cathartic for her. She never thought she would manage to do this, but she doesn't need the reminder of a life she's leaving behind, Gary, high finance and the trappings of wealth that leads to unethical and shallow choices.

Irene was ready to move out of her apartment. And she wondered when she looks out the window of her new place, will she wish she was back there?

The cryptocurrency shares that Gary gambled - they're all gone. She never

Chapter 24

had access to it anyway, she didn't know about the account, and they were ill-gotten gains so whatever he had was confiscated.

So now Gary can't help her. Only she knows she must move forward. Only she can write the new chapter in her life. There's no looking back at this stage. Gary's made his bed; he must lie in it. He is history.

She had thought about moving in with her mum, but relations are a little bit strained with her mum right now, even though they cleared the air after she got her blessing to go and find her mother in Ireland.

However, with her dad now dead, and her mum being a bit uneasy with her choices around Gary, it leaves her needing space.

After all the revelations that came right around that time, she decides to move in with Grace, for the moment anyway. Grace has always looked out for her, and she has a nice place with a spare room.

This will give her some breathing space to decide what to do and then she can decide where she wants to live long term and if she will move, she would like to go traveling for a year, and find her mother and herself at the same time.

Rodney helps her move into Grace's house and he arrives with a removal van one day on his day off.

She thinks it's a very nice gesture for him to help and they order a Chinese takeaway dinner in the evening and have alcohol-free beer because he's driving.

It was their first meal together, she noticed.

And it's very special. It's special because it's in a new place. And it's special because he offered to help her out as a friend.

She really thinks this is the start of something new and special with him and she wants to ask him to kiss her, because he hasn't yet. She doesn't know why he hasn't but suddenly, he leans over, and their hands touch for the first time.

"I really like you Irene," he says quietly. "I know you've been through a tough time lately and I've been trying to give you space to figure it out, but I'd like to spend more time with you. I want to give you as much time as you need, but I really want to kiss you right now, and well, will you let me?"

"Oh, Rodney, I thought you'd never ask. I've been wanting to kiss you since the first time I saw you at the swimming pool, that very first day we met. I knew I could never forgive Gary, but I had to make sure it was real with you. And now it's been months. Yes, Rodney, of course you can kiss me."

In the end, they opened a bottle of wine after the Chinese takeaway and the non-alcoholic beer, and Rodney left the next morning.

Chapter 25

Within a couple of weeks, Rodney asked Irene if she'd like to go away for a short break to one of Europe's capital cities, one time when they have a conversation by the pool. She was back swimming lengths, and he was still doing his community diversion programme. But he needed a break just as much as she did, as he worked very hard.

Irene is completely stunned when he asks her, and she doesn't know what to say. She hasn't left London in a couple of years, except to visit her mother - she's been so concerned with her little bubble and limited world view, that she didn't notice that life was passing her by.

She thinks it's a great idea.

"Which capital city did you have in mind?" she asks, as if that's the most important question she could think of right now.

"I don't know," he says.

"Dublin or Paris, or Berlin I suppose, they're the closest. I'd really like it if you'd come. But only if you don't think it will be weird. I'm having such a lovely time getting to know you these past few weeks. I think it would be lovely to spend a whole weekend together exploring another place."

"Why now?" asked Irene.

"Just to see if we can become more than good friends. I know you've had a hard time with Gary, and what he did is unforgivable. But you deserve someone who treats you better, and I think that's where I come in. Would you like to come out for a smoothie tonight for instance? We could check our schedules and see if there is any time that we can schedule to take a short break? I fancy visiting Dublin this time of year."

"Well, I wouldn't mind a peanut butter smoothie in fairness!"

"And maybe a trip to Dublin would be nice. I have family outside Galway. I could possibly look them up!"

Irene's thoughts raced a mile a minute as she thought of the possibility of going to Ireland for a visit with her mother for the first time. She wouldn't have to tell Rodney the whole story, not until they got there, it was his idea for a holiday, so he probably wouldn't mind.

On second thoughts, no secrets. She would come clean over dinner. She was eating more regularly, now that she was seeing Rodney, and it wasn't a bad thing.

In fact, it was good.

It's good to talk, she thought.

Chapter 26

The first weekend she moved in with Grace, Irene was invited to a party, but she didn't realize until later that it was a Tupperware-selling party.

Rodney took her there expecting a DJ and jukebox tunes, and they laughed about it later over a glass of something cold, even though she felt compelled to buy some new salad boxes.

Rodney is a good influence; he tries to convince her that she can do anything she puts her mind to.

"The hard part is getting started. Once you get started, you can do anything. What is it you want to do?"

"This is the hard part for me. I've tried and I keep failing," she says. She takes a sip of her drink, vodka and cranberry.

"Hey, come on. You can do it," says Rodney and he grabs her hand.

"I've blown through my savings," she says.

"It's all part of the learning curve," says Rodney, "and you're smart and you're beautiful."

He kisses her on the cheek.

In the morning, Irene wakes to the smell of bacon and coffee. She licked her lips and goes downstairs. Grace was up early too, taking care of the housework and prepping breakfast. Irene was grateful for the smell of Grace's lemon-scented tea. They chatted about the party, how it went and how Rodney is a funny guy, but very sweet.

The tea had a yellowish tinge to it, but otherwise it was a normal looking tea served in a China cup. The steam from the hot water and from the cup rose above the table, like a dragon's breath.

The tea was made with fresh lemons and steeped in the fine china tea pot. The morning sun shines through the east window and bleeds over the table. The tea is yellow and amber and clear.

The leaves unfurl in the hot water, letting off a citrus scent, green and bitter and wonderful.

"What are you going to do today?" says Grace.

"I'm going to the library. I'm going to get some books on what to expect travelling to Ireland." She thought again about her mother and didn't say anything. She wondered if she had any siblings.

"Good for you," says Grace. "You can do it," echoing Rodney's words of the previous night.

"I'll be here when you get back."

Irene peers in the window of a discount store on the high street, thinking of Rodney.

On a whim, Irene decides to pop in and see what they have, as she spots a pocket watch in the window for sale that she might like for her first gift to Rodney. These things were important.

"Twenty pounds for each," said the lady at the counter to Irene when she asked how much.

"Twenty pounds," she repeated. Irene doesn't know if she's disappointed or not.

Irene made the sale regardless and the woman took the twenty pounds for the pocket watch into her clenched fist. Irene plans to surprise Rodney with the gold toned trinket later. She thought it would look nice on his shorts as

Chapter 26

he timed the youngsters in the swimming pool as they swam lengths. And not so expensive that he would be worried if it got lost or wet.

The autumn sun was bright, almost blinding. The sky was cloudless, and the air was warm and dry. The London streets were crowded, with people pushing their way towards the central square. It was Friday, the day after payday, but Irene no longer had a job, and no longer a reason to eat gluten free pizza or swim.

Chapter 27

A flight touched down on a warm night into Malaga airport in Spain, two hours past its scheduled arrival time. Irene and Rodney had decided to visit her late father's apartment instead of a capital European city, to explore the place where her future holidays may be spent.

She was glad of Rodney's company on the trip and found many things to like about Andalusia. They hired a car to make the coastal trip from the southern Spanish airport along the south west-coast where the apartment was located at San Pedro de Alcántara.

San Pedro offered a classic Costa del Sol holiday popular with British, European, and Spanish tourists alike, with chic cafés, bars, restaurants, and gift shops lining the beachfront. But Irene soon found out it also had a traditional side. Heading inland from the beach, she was transported to a quaint Spanish village with winding streets, tiny tapas bars, and a market square with old stone buildings and churches.

For a moment, Irene wondered if she could settle here, on this sunny southern frontier so far from home, and get a job at a bar, or a hotel - and

Chapter 27

just swim her days away until she no longer had cobwebs in her head, and her mind was free and clear thinking.

Chapter 28

In Ireland a few weeks later, Irene stepped off the train and onto the platform. It was a small station, and there was no one else around. She looked up and down the tracks, but there was no sign of her mother.

She took a deep breath and tried to calm herself. It was only a misunderstanding. Her mother would be here soon. She looked at the signposts. They were in a language she didn't understand. She didn't know the language.

Was it Irish?

She started to panic. What if she couldn't communicate with her family?

"Excuse me," she said to a woman in a navy coat who was standing on the platform. "Do you speak English?"

The woman looked at Irene in surprise

"Of course, I do, can I help you with something?"

Irene was finding the warmth of the land with the hundred thousand welcomes already, as the woman looked at her kindly, and put her at ease.

Irene let out the breath that she didn't know that she was holding, feeling suddenly foolish. Of course, everyone spoke English in Ireland. She was worrying about nothing.

"My mother's picking me up."

"That's nice. Where are you from?" the woman asked.

"London."

The woman's face broke into a smile. Her accent was lyrical and soft. "Your

Chapter 28

mother will be here soon, I'm sure. She wouldn't leave a girl like you on her own at a train station if you don't know where you're going. There's no need to worry."

Irene nodded and hugged her body to warm herself on the cold platform. She didn't argue with the woman. She was sure that her mother would be here soon. But she felt shaky and sick with nerves. Her mouth was dry, and she felt like she needed to pee.

"I'm sorry," Irene said to the woman. "I don't know what I'm doing here."

"That's all right," the woman said, sensing Irene's discomfort and putting her arm around her shoulders. "You're home now."

Irene looked down at her feet and kicked a stone with the toe of her boot. "I don't know if I'll fit in here," she said quietly. "I don't know if I'll get on with my family."

Before long, a woman of about fifty years old bounded onto the platform and peered around looking for Irene. It was Ciara Finnegan, Irene's mother.

"You're here at last, it's so good to see you," said Ciara, "you must have so many questions. There'll be time for all that later. Come with me, I'll take you back to the house. It's not far."

In the large house, Ciara studied her daughter for a long moment. In the bright light of the kitchen, Irene could see the tired lines around her mother's eyes, which belied her age.

"Irene, you're a bright girl." Ciara said suddenly, "You should go to university. I teach at the local technical college here, and I might be able to get you a place."

Irene shook her head. "I don't want to go to university. I've been to community college and have a diploma in Business. It's served me fine in London."

"You might change your mind." Ciara's voice was gentle. "But there's no rush. You can take a class at the local university. It's a new course in hotel management. I looked it up before you came. I could get you in, as part of my staff privileges. You could work in the hotel here with me while you get to know me, and then maybe go for a job in a bigger hotel when you gain more experience."

"I don't want to go to university," Irene said again. She just wanted to know more about her family, but she could tell this wasn't the time, and that Ciara didn't want to talk about it right now.

Ciara sighed. "Irene, you must make plans," she said. "What about a boyfriend? You're young. You should have fun."

Irene thought about Gary, and she chastised herself. Her thoughts quickly changed to Rodney. "I'm not sure I'm going to have a boyfriend anymore," Irene said. "I've seen how that works with other people. I'm not sure I'm going to do it."

She wasn't sure what she was saying, as she was certainly fond of Rodney, but didn't want to share this with Ciara just yet. The relationship was too young, and she was too conflicted. She was afraid she would spoil things with him if she started to articulate her feelings out loud for another person to hear. She had been hurt so badly in the past.

"You might change your mind," Ciara said again. "There's no rush."

Irene paused and then spoke.

"I love it here. I don't want to leave." Irene held her breath, waiting for her birth mother's response.

"I love it here too," Ciara said, her voice soft. "I was brought up here. But you're young. You might want to go away again at some point. And we've only just met."

"I'll never leave. I promise you." Irene was aware of the desperation in her voice, but she didn't care. She couldn't imagine leaving her mother and this place, not ever. Not now that she has found her.

Ciara smiled sadly. "You don't know that. But I appreciate the sentiment," she said. "And it's great that you want to work here. We can talk about that tomorrow."

"Can I stay here for dinner?" Irene asked, suddenly ravenous. The sea air on the Atlantic seaboard was certainly agreeing with her and she looked forward to whatever was being prepared in the house.

Before long, a meal was prepared, with some sort of pulled pork and mashed potato dish with oven cooked vegetables.

Irene dined at the table; Ciara sat across from her. They laughed and

Chapter 28

shared stories. The table was covered with a dark wool tablecloth and white linen napkins, the china and flatware were ornate and finely crafted, Irene especially liked the dinner knives, the serrated steak knives, the blades etched with a family crest the likes of which she had never seen before, the metal warm to the touch. Finnegan, it must be her mother's family crest

Candles were lit and the refrigerator had been opened, its chill escaping into the room. Irene could smell the scent of the food on her olfactory glands.

Irene was not fully sure of what she was eating, but it was warm and delicious, and she felt at home and relaxed and at peace with herself. And her mother.

Ciara takes Irene's hand while they are eating, and they sit silently, not needing to speak. It is all so strange, yet so wonderful.

The touch of home, she thinks, is her mother's touch. It is soft, but firm and certain.

During the previous week, Irene had been in Ireland, and she had woken early and lay in bed in her room for a while in the small hotel that her Irish family ran, thinking about what she should do. She could stay in Ireland, of course. It wasn't a million miles away from London, and she had never lived abroad before, so it might just suit her.

She was also very hopeful that things would work out well with her birth family. She had a younger sister, Cliona, and her birth mum's name was Ciara, who gave birth to her when she was seventeen years old.

The day after they met, Ciara had offered Irene a job in the small family run hotel, and Irene was conflicted. She looked around at the pale cream walls, the deep green carpet, the mahogany brown fabric on the armchairs and sofas, a little dismayed at the dilapidation, but excited, nonetheless.

The hotel was a two-story building with outbuildings, made of stone, on a quiet country road, nestled within trees and hedgerows, with a rear parking lot and a large front drive. There were orchards to the rear side and an abundance of wildlife, coupled with the family's three dogs and two cats.

She was torn between wanting to stay here and experience new things and the fear of being too far away from her family and the only home she had ever known. It was a big decision to make, and she had no idea what to do.

She could easily afford to stay in Ireland for weeks if she wanted to, but she still wasn't sure she was ready to stay here for any length of time, but she had the excuse that her flight was booked to return the following week. It was a flexible flight, and easy to change, but she didn't want to admit that to herself. Not yet.

She almost thought about posting a message on Facebook to ask her friends what they thought, but she wasn't sure what she would say.

How did you say "I've just found my birth mum, and I'm thinking of staying in Ireland" in a way that didn't sound like a midlife crisis? She knew they would think she was crazy.

She eventually got out of bed, showered, and dressed in her usual jeans, t-shirt, and leather jacket, and went out for breakfast. These were her casual clothes, as she had to dress smartly for the office in London, but that was so far away now.

She had decided to go for a walk around the village to clear her head, so she grabbed her backpack and headed outside. It was a grey day, so she walked through the village with her head down, lost in thought. She didn't notice that someone was following her until they bumped into her.

"I'm so sorry," a man said, as Irene turned around. "You're new around here or are you just here for a visit?" he probed.

"Just visiting," Irene said, suddenly self-conscious.

Rodney and Irene texted each other all the time, but they only called once in the week, on Sunday.

Irene was happy in Ireland for the week she was away, but she missed Rodney more than she could have ever imagined.

She loved the freedom of being away from London and all the drama she had left behind, but she also loved hearing Rodney's voice on the phone.

How could she reconcile this into her future, she wondered? Now that she has some finances to do it, she might stay in Ireland for a while, she thinks. Or at least go back to London and think about it with some distance to ponder her plans. And of course, discuss it with Rodney.

The week passed slowly, but eventually the day came when Irene decided to return to London. She was looking forward to seeing Rodney again, but she

Chapter 28

was sad to say goodbye to Ireland, her mother Ciara, and her eight-year-old half-sister Cliona as well. She wondered if she had made the right choice in coming back.

Chapter 29

Irene arrived back in London on a cold, grey December day. The train from Galway, and then the flight and travel through the airport was tiring, and Irene was anxious to see Rodney again. She took a taxi home, but when she arrived, she found that the door to the apartment was locked. She rang the bell, but there was no answer.

Irene found that she didn't have the keys to Grace's apartment on her, so she sat down on the steps to wait. She telephoned Rodney to see if he would like to come and pick her up. She wondered if he had gone away for the weekend, but she knew that he hadn't mentioned any plans.

Irene waited for more than an hour before Rodney finally called over. He was carrying a brown paper bag and a small cardboard box. Irene could tell that he was surprised to see her sitting on the stairs unable to get into the flat.

"Hey," he said, "how was your travel from Ireland?"

"It was fine," said Irene. I'm a bit tired because I had to travel by train as well as the flight. I hope you don't mind that I've come back without giving you any warning."

"No, of course not," Rodney said. "I'm glad to see you."

Later that week, Rodney leaned back in his chair at the station and stretched his arms over his head. It had been a long frustrating day.

He had never felt so helpless in his life. He was used to being in control, to having all the answers. But this time, he had been at the mercy of the

Chapter 29

computer algorithms which caused his program to crash, and he lost half a day's work because of it.

He looked out the window and saw that it was getting dark. He had been so engrossed in work that he had not realized that the day had ended. He looked at his watch and saw that it was almost 8 p.m.

He was tired and hungry, but he was hoping that Irene would call to see how his day had been. He wanted to hear her voice, to tell her all about it.

He could hear his stomach growling as he sat there waiting for a call. He got up and went to the kitchen in the station. He opened the refrigerator and pulled out a container of leftovers. The rich, spicy scent of Chinese food, the aroma of rich teriyaki sauce.

The food reminded him of the restaurant where he and Irene had eaten the night before. The chicken was still warm, and he could smell the sauce.

He was about to heat it up when his phone rang.

With his work of the last few weeks, he had secured a win for the Metropolitan police and a promotion for himself. He should have been celebrating, but instead he was driving home exhausted, his mind spinning.

If he was being honest with himself, he would admit that he was relieved it was all over. The pressure of the last few weeks had been too much.

He was so tired that he almost missed the turnoff for his avenue. He cursed under his breath and swerved into the parking space, barely braking in time to avoid hitting the side of the apartment building.

He went into the kitchen and made coffee, taking a sip of the hot brew as he leaned against the counter. He closed his eyes, enjoying the warmth of the cup in his hands, and thought back to the last time he had been here.

He plated up the warm teriyaki chicken and ate it hungrily, as if he hadn't eaten since last night.

He always thought of himself as a career police officer. It was all he ever wanted to do. But lately, he'd been spending more time with Irene. And the more he spent time with her, the more he realized that maybe he didn't deserve the single, bachelor's life. Maybe he could be happy with somebody else, maybe even married.

And maybe he didn't need to be married to the job. Not all the time anyway.

Maybe he had other choices.

It was a Sunday night, and he was on duty. He was sure Irene was home, but he wasn't sure he was going to call her. He was waiting for her to call him. She had to be the one to call him.

He felt a little guilty, a little ashamed. He knew that he was being manipulative. But he couldn't help himself. He wanted her to call him. He wanted her to be the one to make the first move. He felt as though he had made some big moves himself, now he wanted her to make a move.

Irene was famous for being too busy to make the first move.

He took a sip from his coffee and thought about her again. She was so accomplished, and so independent. She could do whatever she wanted to do. Whenever she wanted to do it.

What did she want, this feisty young lady who had come into his life so unexpectedly? He had no idea. And that was part of her charm. He suspected that if he did know what she wanted, he might lose interest in her, as was often the case in his relationships with women.

He smiled at the thought of what his friends would say if they knew why he was not calling her. They would tell him that it was unwise, and a plan doomed to fail.

Don't call her, you're on duty. Make her sweat! And they'd be right, of course. Still, he couldn't help himself. Soon, the thought would go right out of his head as he was interrupted. He reached for the phone and saw Irene's name flashing on the screen.

"Irene," he said as he answered the call. "How are you?" he gushed.

"Hi, Rodney," she said.

"I'm really glad you called me," said Rodney.

"You are? I was hoping you would call me," Irene said with a smile in her voice. "I just wanted to see how your evening was going."

"It has been great," Rodney said with affection in his voice. But unfortunately, they were soon interrupted, and they were not able to catch up that night.

The radio buzzed, and Rodney picked up the microphone. "Go ahead," he said.

Chapter 29

"There's a report of a carjacking on the Common. Can you assist?"

"Yes, Sergeant," said Rodney, as he grabbed his gear and left the chicken leftovers on the counter, uneaten.

Chapter 30

"Hey," Irene said to Rodney the next time she saw him. She had called around to his apartment.

"Hey." Rodney leaned in and kissed Irene. "Are you okay?"

"I'm good. I just wanted to see you," said Irene.

"Do you want to come in?"

"I do."

Rodney put his arm around her.

"How was Ireland? We never really got a chance to talk about it since you got back. There was a car-jacking on Sunday night when you phoned, so sorry I couldn't talk then."

"It was nice. I've never been to Ireland before. It's beautiful, but it's hard to know what I think of it."

"Did you meet your family?"

"I did. It was interesting."

"How come?" Rodney asked. "What was it like?"

"You know, the way families are, I suppose. They love me, but it's a different kind of love than I thought it would be," Irene replied

"How do you mean?"

"Well, it's hard to explain. They're a little like strangers, but they're also family. And they're just so different, you know?"

Chapter 30

Rodney nodded. "Yes."

"And they're from a small town in the middle of nowhere," Irene shrugged at the memory of the fields of cows and horses on the road to the closest town where she got off the train. "It's just not what I thought it would be."

"What did you think it would be like?"

"I don't know. I thought there would be more of a connection between me and the place. But there isn't."

Irene shook her head, and a lock of hair fell into her face, disappointed.

She continued, "Maybe it's my fault that there isn't a connection; I don't know."

"But how could it be your fault?" said Rodney, "you were only a baby when you were adopted by your family here in London. I can't imagine how difficult that must be for you, finding that out now."

"Oh, I always knew, I just had such high expectations of meeting my birth mother. But I do have a sister, and my mother Ciara is young, so that's something. We have a lot of time to catch up on. But I'm just not sure they want me in their lives, or if it was such a shock."

Rodney's brother, who he had been looking after to the greatest extent possible in London, is doing much better in terms of services and no longer needs his support all the time. The extra community programs he has been doing with the swimming and the disadvantaged youth, and the cyber-crime training with the police force, means he is in high demand in terms of jobs, and he secures a welcome offer of a job in Ireland.

"I've got a job offer," Rodney says suddenly to Irene.

"What? I didn't know you were even looking?"

"In Ireland."

"That's great! We can live together or make plans. Is that why you were looking in Ireland?"

Irene is excited suddenly, and then cautious, seeming that she did not wanting to reveal too much about her feelings.

"Yes. I don't need to take care of my brother so much now. He doesn't need me anymore now he's older. I'm a lot less tied down than I had been."

"That's great news."

"I had been looking after my brother in recent times, as you know. But he is doing better now. He has services. And his medication is working. He is doing so well that the social workers were looking into getting him into a group home. I am so proud of him. I had been so afraid that he would end up back in the hospital or worse. I had been afraid that I would lose him again."

"That's great," Irene said. "That's really great," she said again.

"Yeah, it is. It's been a long time coming, but we are enormously proud of him."

"Are you going to take the job in Ireland?" Irene asked.

"I don't know." Rodney, it appears, was just as indecisive as Irene.

"Why not?" she asked.

"I don't know if I want to be in Ireland."

"You don't want to be near me?" Irene was shocked.

"That's not it."

"Then what is it?"

He didn't say anything. He didn't have to say anything. Irene could read the answer in his eyes. He wasn't sure if he wanted to go away to be near her anymore. He didn't want to be Irene's partner.

But Rodney was just thinking about his brother. He had to compartmentalize his feelings and it wasn't easy, because his brother was a big part of his life and the thought of moving to Ireland for Irene and a new job was really a big deal. He didn't know if Irene's new life in Ireland would work out either, or then where would they both be?

Stranded abroad, unhappy, and possibly without a decent foundation on which to build a future.

And yet, it was only Ireland, not that far away. Not so far away that they couldn't come home.

When Rodney had told his brother about the new job, he was just focused on himself and his place in the group home. He didn't want Rodney to be a part of his daily life anymore.

He didn't want to depend on Rodney anymore. And not because of anger or lack of gratitude, exactly the opposite. He completely understood the freedoms that being in a group home would bring him.

Chapter 30

"Rodney," Irene said, "I want to do something. I want to just take a year off and travel and see if I can make a connection with my family. Maybe work in the hotel and do a course like my mother suggested. Maybe make a real connection.

"After what happened with Gary, and then after, me in the hospital and my dad dying. It's given me some perspective. I don't want to work in unsatisfying jobs for the rest of my life. I'm tired of it."

"Irene, you can't just give up on London like that," Rodney said. "What about us?"

"I was thinking maybe I could borrow some money from my inheritance," Irene said.

She continued. "I want to do this. I can't tell you how much I want to do this. It's been eating me up that I don't know my birth family. I just want to take a year and travel and get to know them. There are jobs in Ireland too, you know."

"Irene, I wish you the best, I really do," Rodney said. If you must do this, you have my blessing. But I don't think you should do it this way. Do you know what I mean? If you really want to do this, then get a job as a travel agent. Do something that will give you the time to do what you want and still be able to live, but maybe just not away from home."

"I don't know if there's such a job," Irene said.

"You haven't even looked into it?" Rodney said. "I thought you wanted to do this so badly, you would do anything."

"I was so sure it was going to be easy," Irene said.

"Well, if you want my opinion, Irene, I think you need to think very carefully," Rodney said. "You mightn't form a close bond with your family anytime soon, and if you're not careful, you're going to lose all your capital unless you get another job. Why would you leave London?"

"But Rodney, you've been offered a job in Dublin! Aren't you going to take it?" Irene said.

"You're right Irene, I know how much this means to you. I could come with you. I do have a job offer in Dublin, and you can connect with your family in the west of the country on the weekends or on holidays. It might be less pressure on all of you. You don't have to stay in a dreary hotel in the West of Ireland baking scones."

"Yes, maybe you're right."

Rodney looked into her eyes and said the words that would change everything.

He really wasn't sure about leaving his job in the police force in London, and he was conflicted about taking a job offer in another country.

But perhaps I want to bake scones, Irene thought. *That's my choice to make or not.*

"If that's what you want, I'll go for a long time without you. I'll wait for you to come back if you want me to. I'll try out a long-distance relationship to see if it would work. Just as friends or if you wanted more, then I could certainly try that too. One thing's for sure, you need financial advice on what to do with the money that you got when your father passed. You need more advice than I can give you."

Rodney had never felt so alone as he said those words. He knew what he was saying.

The woman he loved could walk out on him for good and he could not do anything about it. He had no fight left in him. He had no more words.

Irene had been frozen in time listening to Rodney. She was glad that he had finally said what he needed to say. But she knew that it would not change anything.

She still wanted to be with him, and she longed for him, but in the end, it was her decision about leaving, and it was time for her to utterly understand that everything that happens is for a reason.

After a long silence, Irene finally responded to Rodney.

"I know you mean well with everything you're saying, but I'm just not sure. If I stay in London, there are always going to be questions in my head about my mum and my birth family. If I go to Dublin, it might be the same and I won't connect either. I'm sorry, Rodney."

Rodney just looked at her and said the only thing that he could say. "I understand."

He then looked at Irene and tried to smile, but it was not easy for him. He looked

Chapter 30

at her one last time and turned around and walked away from her without looking back.

Post Script

Four years later, Irene's plane touches down at Heathrow Airport, and Ciara and Cliona are with her. They haven't been in the habit of travelling together, except into Galway city and on the train to Dublin occasionally. Irene now runs the family hotel and has completed her master's in business from the technical university where her mother teaches.

Irene is immensely chuffed with herself at graduation, as it is a degree that only a few years ago she would barely admit she wanted.

Now a confident young woman approaching thirty, she hasn't had an anxiety attack in years, and she attributes this to cold-water swims and running on the beach on the Atlantic Seaboard.

She has long since reconciled with Rodney, now an Inspector, and they have a wonderful if non-traditional relationship where they meet in Andalusia for holidays every six weeks and talk on the phone and text the rest of the time. It's not what most couples do, but it suits their lifestyle.

Thank goodness for good broadband service!

At the airport to meet Irene and her mother Ciara and sister Cliona, are Irene's mum from London, and her younger sister who is now a lawyer. Irene is extremely excited to see them and there are hugs all round as they are re-acquainted.

Irene smiles at the memory of buying the laptop for her sister for six hundred pounds which helped her on her way starting to study, back when Irene was a real estate secretary, all those years ago. It seems like a lifetime ago.

Gary set up his own tech startup company in recent times, Irene hears through a mutual friend, and Julia is collaborating with him in it as an interpreter. They now live as a small family unit, with Gary, Julia and Rosie, in a council flat in Greenwich Village – Gary no longer practices law.

As for Suzanne, rumour has it that she has gone to Dubai after leaving prison and is working on some business deals out there.

Printed in Poland
by Amazon Fulfillment
Poland Sp. z o.o., Wrocław
04 April 2023

de1a812f-fd40-42ad-ac47-253788256876R02